HE LANDS IN PALM SPRINGS

A Father Tierney Novel

John Shekleton

He Lands in Palm Springs

ISBN: 978-1-935751-68-7 (Print)
ISBN: 978-1-935751-67-0 (ePub)

Mo Keijuk Press
mokeijukpress@AOL.com
Printed in the U.S.A.

Many come to the desert to revive their souls,
to reawaken the spirit that has fallen asleep in other climates.

Chapter 1

Joe clicked through a mental checklist one more time. He knew how to organize himself. Organizing was calming art; it steadied him when panic struck.

Yes, he had taken his morning meds and packed the rest in his backpack, now safely stowed behind his seat. Yes, he had rummaged through the Las Vegas motel room's dresser drawers. They were empty except for a phone directory and the Gideon's Bible whose untouched presence had rebuked him this morning.

He adjusted the mirrors. He was ready to go. He closed his eyes and uttered a silent prayer—no words, only want. Fr. Joseph Tierney, recently HIV positive and AWOL from his once-formidable life as pastor of Mater Dei, a large urban Catholic parish, was heading into a new land. He needed angels to accompany him. Legions of them.

Joe pulled out of the motel parking lot at 6 a.m. and made for the I-15. He stifled a yawn. He had risen before dawn to get into Palm Springs by midmorning, and he felt tired after a night of uneasy sleep. Last night, perhaps more intensely than any of the other nights on this trip, thoughts of his ex, Kenny O'Connor, made a satyr's den of his psyche. His tendons had seemed to vibrate, and his pent-up sexual energy had ripped through all his muscles.

Joe came to a stop sign at Charleston Boulevard and smiled for the first time that day. Soon he would be a few hour's drive away from his old flame, who now worked as an electrician at Camp Pendleton near

San Diego. Things had changed in Kenny's life. He, too, had learned he was HIV. And he was seeing someone.

But what could that mean? Seeing someone. Kenny was Joe's beacon of hope. Joe wasn't going to let any coastal fog obscure it. Joe believed in "meant to be," and Kenny was meant for him as he was meant for Kenny. Their months together proved it. A vigorous twenty-nine year old with an in-shape thirty-six year old. They were different in many ways, yet both were jeans and t-shirts guys, Midwestern pinups, and comfortable with each other. Only Joe's reluctance had ended their relationship.

But, before contacting Kenny, Joe had to get to the Palm Springs guesthouse where he could finally start to straighten out the curved mountain drive his life had become. His one HIV-positive friend, elegant and gay Episcopal priest Edward Brockton, was friends with the guesthouse owners. Edward—fifty, fit, and topped with a head of thick gray hair—had a large cadre of friends. He had made a call and gotten Joe both a job at the guesthouse, Casa Vista Oro, and secured a place for him to stay in a cheap, predominantly gay rental complex nearby. Thank God for friends with connections and the willingness to use them.

Joe kept the thought of Edward's kindness in mind as he drove on. He was intent on proving Edward's trust. He'd work hard, clean toilets, Pine-Sol the floors, trim bougainvillea, smile at guests, nod, and look pretty. He'd be on time and stay late. Edward would be proud of him. And he would have a paycheck, his first nonchurch paycheck in over a decade.

Joe assured himself he wasn't running from trouble, the way his best friend Pascal had put it. Joe knew he couldn't run from a pain that lived off the central artery of his soul. Besides, Joe hoped to find peace focusing his soul on simpler issues like sparkling clean floors or mirrors without smudges. And in another city, nearer his dreamboat guy. Joe did feel a tiny whisk of fear about moving to Palm Springs, a city brimming with gay folk. He was a "non-scene" guy, as Pascal had put it. But didn't he already have gay friends, Edward and Pascal, both nurturing and kind to him? He knew he could make more, maybe a set of friends to fill his life. To fill up the loss of Kenny, if his beloved remained lost.

Maybe even friends to help fight off the nagging power of shame that had insisted on traveling with him.

Joe pulled off the freeway to fill the tank. He sighed and shook his head in dismay as the dollars rolled on and up. He was running through the cash the Darlings had given him. He needed to be careful. He didn't want to go back to their deep pockets again; the idea made him sweat. At least he had three months' worth of meds, the one essential. The machine clanged, and his tank was full.

By 7:30 a.m., Joe was deep in the desert speeding over seemingly limitless flat concrete. He kept changing radio channels from stations with Mexican news chatter, pleased that the accent he'd learned from his *mamá* and *abuelita* was the same he heard here.

Now he was ready for the final leg. If he could have, he'd have rocketed to Palm Springs. That's what he'd been back home. A rocketeer. A rising star.

* * *

Cyril Anastasis rose early, excited about the new man coming to work. He did his best not to wake Matt by rolling carefully out of bed, softly closing the bathroom door, and keeping the lights off. They had argued last night about the wisdom of taking on an unknown individual. Cy didn't want an early morning reenactment of that scene. Best to let Matt sleep. Cy had pushed hard last night, maybe too hard. But this case dug into him. Cy was the grandson of a Greek Orthodox priest. He was the nephew of a priest. He loved priests and their souls. They reminded him of his own.

Cy had once helped Edward Brockton recover from his divorce—helped a little too fervently, too intimately. But Edward was now only a friend, and he had called seeking help for a friend of his, another priest in need.

Fully dressed, Cy quietly left Matt and crossed a courtyard to the office. Inside the office, he booted up the computer, which seemed to take longer each day, and then went out to check on the fish in the koi pond. Looking into the water, he felt a calm surety enter his body.

Then he looked around. Everything he saw pleased him: the high white walls, the saltwater pool, the inground spa with seating for eight, the stand of five cypresses along the roadside wall, the matching Mexican fan palms at the guesthouse entrance, and the bed of well-tended annuals and agave. The landscape said refinement. Refinement and taste. Refinement, taste, and exclusivity. That's what Cy's clientele wanted.

Satisfied that his domain was flourishing in the early morning's kind light, Cy headed around the corner to open up the small guesthouse kitchen. Their manager was on vacation, and it was Cy's job to put together breakfast.

The morning was unusually cool for a summer day, but Cy enjoyed it. It woke him up, made his fifty-five-year-old muscles flex to gain warmth. Work in his family's delis had molded him into a morning person. When he became manager of their Greenwich Village deli, Gardens of Salonika, in 1973, he would stumble into the subway by 4 a.m. six days a week, even if he'd spent most of the night dancing or at the baths. He was a spinning disco ball of energy in those days. He still was, he thought, though with diminishing revolutions and loss of a few mirrored tiles. He chuckled at the thought.

Chapter 2

Kenny groaned as he struggled to toss off a boozy sleep. He reached over to slap his hand onto the alarm's stop button, hitting it spot-on the third time. He shifted up and lifted his legs over the edge of the bed, remembering to crunch his abs as he moved. Then he waited, still groggy.

A couple of months ago he would have sprung out of bed, happy to be in Southern California, grateful for a job on the Marine Air Station Camp Pendleton surrounded by squadrons of men with tight bodies and sculpted jaws.

But then he'd gotten the phone call from Joe Tierney, and every pool of happiness drained away. The call had left him scurrying to get an HIV test.

It came back positive.

Within minutes of that news, the panic set in. Then came dull dread. And these days, a fear of rejection. Kenny had only told one man, Jasper.

But this morning Joe, his ex, was on his mind.

They'd had a genuine connection, more than a hookup. Kenny's first real, adult relationship. Everything was going well for them until Joe had that "I'm a priest" moment and fled from the relationship, damming up all access channels. Kenny's new pals in California had told him he was lucky. "A guy like that can be a pain to live with. It's always risky. He's really married to an idea. An ideal."

Kenny wasn't averse to "risky." His prediagnosis sex life proved it. For a moment, that awareness nearly stopped his heart. He lowered his head left then right to stretch his trapezius muscles. He looked up and breathed deeply. He had really fucked up. And he'd fucked up Joe.

Kenny sat silently a few more minutes. Then he stood up and ran his hands over his blond buzz cut. He reminded himself he had one solid thing that anchored him now. He was seeing someone again.

Second Lieutenant Jasper Wylands, U.S.M.C., African American and driven to achieve, to be in command-the type of man Kenny lusted after. They'd nodded at each other on base one day, spoken together at the San Diego Eagle on a uniform and gear night.

Jasper might be the one. Jasper had stuck with him through his diagnosis, through the pain and fear. He'd held him when Kenny thought he'd never feel another man's skin again. And Jasper wanted him, craved him. Kenny knew this as much as he knew what tool to use for any job.

Kenny lifted his arms to smell his pits. He was okay. He had an outdoor job today anyway. The stench would be wafting off him by ten. He decided only to brush his teeth and leave the stubble on his face. Jasper liked that. Maybe he'd wander by today.

Then he remembered. Joe was nearly here. In California. Kenny was supposed to see him for the first time since their split, and he didn't know if he was brave enough for that encounter. It was sure to be awkward, messy. Things hadn't ended well. The pain had driven Kenny to California to start anew. He had felt discarded. Tossed away after a wiser—or grimmer—specter took over Joe.

And now there was the virus. How could Joe want to see him again?

And there was the issue of amends. Some parental form within him kept goading Kenny to make it, to say it. But with what words?

It was ten, and the sweat was streaming off Kenny. His crew was digging today, checking an old buried cable for damage sustained when a caravan of LVS, which he now knew meant Logistics Vehicle System, was hauling sand and rock for a couple of days. They'd have to dig down to discover what caused the wires to go unstable. It wasn't as great a job as working on the MCTSSA nerve center, a cool accumulation of computers and servers for tactical support that required vast amounts of wiring. Working there was a plum job and required a step-above skill set. His reward was being surrounded by a staff of the fittest desk jockeys on base, a company that included Jasper.

Kenny stopped to stand up straight. Wiping his brow with his shirt sleeve, he thought again of Joe. Joe's cross-country move complicated things. Kenny hadn't even told Jasper about his ex's imminent arrival.

Kenny bent down to examine the soil. He needed to test the back-fill thermal properties. He glanced up and over at Jorge, the scrawny grunt assigned to help him. Jorge had taken off his shirt. Kenny stared too long and felt the movement in his crotch. Jorge's form was so familiar. Just like Joe's.

Kenny looked down again to peer into the trench. He didn't want anyone to notice his bulge. Damn! Damn! Two guys pulled him. Only one of them was HIV, which seemed a softer place now, a comfortable place to touch down.

He gripped the handle of the shovel and dug like a fiend.

* * *

Jasper Wylands always wanted to be a hero. But a living hero, not a faint memory in history, a plaque, or a statue. He had learned in his training that surviving was a key objective in any heroic action; it just wasn't the absolute, primary goal. In any case, heroic acts often left you cut hard and deep by a blade you didn't see coming.

The problem was Jasper had started to see Kenny as the blade wielder. Kenny would ambush you. He was the sniper behind you, the gun in the open window. This development in their relationship made Jasper want to pound his head into the poured concrete of his office wall. He had fallen hard for the blond babe from the Midwest and even concocted a storyline of what a life might be like without all the sneaking around. Two guys and their dogs and their gear, tromping through life.

Kenny had seemed so normal and masculine, the words Jasper used in his online profiles to describe his ideal match—the profiles that only displayed his six-pack and the curling hairs above his thick cock. He was a first lieutenant in the Marine Corps and could get trashed for being gay. But he had needs. Then one day Kenny showed up for duty. And he wasn't a member of the Green Machine. He was civilian and not in his command, so free to engage.

It didn't take long. Some talk about Green Bay, the Colts, and the Bears—typical Midwestern bonding crap. They went out a few days after for a couple of beers. Kenny told him that he had suspected. Not having to do with any mannerism or comment, no lisp or swish. Just the intensity of Jasper's smile and the way Jasper liked to watch him move and bend while he pulled wires and connected up distribution boards.

Jasper swung his chair around to look outside toward the vehicle storage buildings. Kenny was out there today, sweating in the sun. Jasper could go out to look but didn't want to draw anyone's attention. He had reports to review not an inspection to perform. But he wanted to see Kenny, to keep on reminding himself why it was important to stay open.

Jasper closed his eyes and clenched his fists, his childlike version of anger control. He hated it. He was the man who could fix anything. A degree in electrical engineering, now a liaison to the defense contractors building tactical systems. But this! He hated that he could do nothing about it. Kenny had the disease. It would never go away. It would stay inside him and eat away at him. Eat away at his newfound friend. His newfound love.

Could Jasper remain proud and strong in that relationship?

He opened his eyes and unclenched his fists, untensed his body. He rubbed one of his ribs, the one bruised in last week's training exercise. The massage didn't help. The pain surrounding his chest remained.

* * *

It was noon and time for chow. Kenny planned to run into Jasper at the Stateside Café, their meet-up spot on first Fridays. He knew that the gnawing in his stomach wasn't hunger. Kenny had one more secret to reveal. The secret about Joe's driving into town today. Well, not into San Diego, but close enough. Over into Palm Springs. He wished he could have a beer or two before launching into what was becoming a soap opera existence.

They arrived at the same time and tossed a quick fist bump. Jasper insisted on no hugging in public. Kenny had no problem with that rule. He wasn't one for public displays anyway. Maybe a thump on the shoulder or a tap on the bum, but nothing more.

Kenny wiped his brow as they sat down in one of the isolated booths at the back with no views and few neighboring diners, all high-backed chambers for private talk. These were the spots for personal business, for friendly warnings or soft rebukes. Base personnel respected the secrecy protocol that covered them.

These booths weren't their normal spot, but today Kenny knew his words could whip up anger and bruise their relationship more. He had headed off to the back and a clearly reluctant Jasper had slowly and hesitantly followed.

Kenny ordered his usual tuna melt and Jasper had his regular salad, dressing on the side. The man was serious about his physique, and Kenny liked a man with form.

"You've got something on your mind?" Jasper asked, forking around for a grape tomato. He obviously didn't like eating back here. He hadn't said much of anything. There was heat in his voice. They were supposed to plan their weekend, except Kenny couldn't, for sure, plan this weekend. Kenny needed to factor in the new variable that was probably soon ready to slip into the Coachella Valley.

Putting down his sandwich, Kenny wiped his lips with his napkin. He'd just say it. He wasn't much for a lot of words. He steadied his eyes on Jasper.

"Joe, my ex from back home, is coming today." Kenny gulped. "Not here, but to Palm Springs."

Jasper was still. The air in the booth seemed to vanish. "He's on vacation?"

Kenny shifted on the bench. "No, no," he said, shaking his head.

"I should've told you. He's moving to Palm Springs. He's got a job there. He's going to call me when he gets in."

Jasper's head lowered to the left, a sure sign to Kenny that a battalion of questions was mustering behind his eyes. "He got a parish there?"

Question two. Good one. On target. Why is he coming?

Kenny shook his head and looked down. This conversation was far more difficult than he had expected. Was it because of the delicate uncertainty that he knew lay inside his heart?

"He's not a priest anymore, I guess. I don't really understand it all. And I should've told you sooner. He called a couple of weeks ago." Kenny stopped to examine Jasper's eyes. They were cool, still, an analytical chestnut without too much of an anger buzz. "He said he'd decided to make a change in his life, to explore his sexuality. You know, the sort of language you get from someone who's been in the closet. You've heard it. No?"

Kenny hoped that last question, the generic coming out one, would take this conversation onto a therapeutic route. It was something he'd read online from some Dr. Whatzu's website. He had been trying to learn how to talk about these things, these feelings of repression and fear, the feelings that had rarely visited him before a month ago when he had been happy.

Jasper just nodded. He pulled his hands into his lap so Kenny couldn't see them. "What does it all mean?" he asked.

Kenny inhaled, deep enough to lift his chest. He held that pocket of air a second and resisted the urge to crack his knuckles and brew up a way to dodge the question. He didn't want to go hiding down the butch rabbit hole, just smiling and saying "I don't know." Joe had talked to him about doing that, tweaking his big ears. Butch rabbit hole. Everyone he knew seemed to be comfortable there.

"First off, I am truly sorry I didn't tell you right away about Joe's decision to come to California. I know it has implications because we are together."

Kenny paused to assess how he was doing. Jasper's mood was hard to read. Maybe he was locking into Marine mode.

"But Joe and I are over, babe. I'm with you now. I want to be with you now." Kenny moved a foot under the table to tap Jasper's left boot.

"But you're planning to see him, I assume," Jasper said.

Yeah, there was anger in Jasper's voice, the vibration he might produce for a new recruit with a serious fuck-up. Kenny had heard it once. He knew where it could head.

"I have to see him," Kenny said, opening his arms a bit, a welcoming gesture. "He's coming all the way here to see me. I know that. He wants to see if we can get back together, although he hasn't said that yet. But I can guess. I've told him about you. Really, I have."

"And what did you say about me?"

"That I was seeing a really great guy at Camp Pendleton."

"Seeing?"

Kenny's face reddened with frustration. "I said 'seeing' to Joe, but he knows what that means. I could tell in his voice, or rather, in his quiet. He became distant, I mean, sounded distant. And *you* know what I meant. What 'seeing' means. With us."

Kenny stopped a second. He wanted to reach over and hold Jasper's hand. He leaned in, laid his arms on the table palms up. "You didn't cut me off when I found out I was positive. You said you wanted to keep going with me. We've got something, the two of us. We get each other. I like that, and I don't want to lose it. Really, babe."

Kenny fought the urge to grab ahold of Jasper, but Jasper stayed rigid with his command face fully furled.

Kenny sat back to wait. He was exhausted now. Last night, when he couldn't sleep, he'd drunk himself into a stupor. He had begged off a night at Jasper's, knowing he'd have to think through this confession about Joe.

"Let me put it this way," Jasper said, nearly whispering. "I don't want to get my feelings more mashed up than they are. We're still adjusting to your...your status. So far, so good. But this priest..." Jasper shook his head. His face turned sour. Then he drew a deep breath and leaned back into the booth. "You've got to see him, of course. To avoid him would be cowardly."

Kenny's shoulders relaxed a bit. And they both smiled.

"Okay, let's go. I have reports to review," Jasper said as he picked up his check and shifted out of the booth.

Chapter 3

Joe had passed a parade of giant wind turbines and was rounding a rocky outcrop, heading from I-10 into Palm Springs. The mountain was now a hovering mass, there on his right. The air-conditioner in his Honda struggled as the sun baked the bleached-out landscape. It was blistering outside, and the mountain's slopes appeared dry and harsh. Primeval, almost, so old and so formidable.

He had passed a couple of desolate housing outposts and started to wonder what he was getting into. Then came hints of a bigger town and the normal signs of an American roadway. It could've been the rural Midwest, except for the lack of brick and the presence of palm trees that began to punctuate the horizon. Soon palms were everywhere. Two or three together, like a family or friends out for a chat. And there were hedges of flowering plants. And some weird flowering shrub with orange-red and gold blossoms and feathered greenery. Joe started to smile. He started to relax. Things grew here. There must be water under this dryness. He'd be able to survive in Palm Springs just like these plants, which were the signposts of a nurturing society, no?

Joe pulled over on Alejo after he'd glanced at, what seemed to be, a coffee shop named Koffi. He needed to get out, stretch the limbs he now realized were tense from days of car travel. Finding parking was easy. Few people were out. He took a spot in a large parking lot, sat a second, then got out. He quickly reached back in to get his sunglasses and a cap. As he turned, he saw he'd driven past a little church.

It looked Catholic. Two niches held statues: Mary in one and Jesus with his hands raised in blessing in the other. The building was white-washed with thick walls. He wondered whether the inside was sticky and moist, full of the sweat of parishioners. He smiled. Funny that his first stop in Palm Springs would bring him feet from an altar.

Joe walked to the road and found a path that led into an open courtyard planted with trees and grass, watched over by a huge statue of Don Quixote. Quest imagery. That was a good sign.

Joe hurried over to the coffee shop and opened the door into a small cool space. The heads of several lone gentlemen sipping their midmorning brew popped up, unashamedly keeping their gaze on him as he walked to the counter.

The young barista, with scruffy beard and tattoos winding up both arms, served Joe a small cup of their strongest brew accompanied by a wink. Joe left his change for a tip and smiled back, wondering if the wink was an invitation to conversation. He was unaccustomed to winking, or maybe his facial muscles were frozen, like a lot of his emotional machinery. Winking wasn't a skill a priest cultivated in these days of misdeeds and misdirection. He sauntered back toward the court-yard, still evaluating the interaction with the cute barista. He picked up a *Desert Daily Guide* at the door and found a wooden chair under a tree. Birds were busy on the ground pecking for something Joe's eyes couldn't see. He set the coffee and *Guide* down and settled into the comforting slats, letting his body relax. It was hot, but under the shade, it felt okay. There was even a breeze that played tag with him. He was here. He was in his new spot, Palm Springs. He felt good.

Joe looked up at the massive mountain slopes, which seemed to compel his attention. *It must be a furnace up there,* he thought. Just as he lifted his cup, another figure entered the courtyard. A young man in a yellow tank top and green gym shorts, no hat, skin brown like a Mexican's. He was chatting on his phone. He passed by Joe and gave him a head nod, telling his friend in Spanish he'd spotted *un guapo* with searching eyes sitting under the tree.

This attention made Joe feel good. He had always been an attractor, like a magnet, the holy man to watch. He had energy and daring.

And now... Look at him. He'd thrown away his career to follow his gut—or his heart. He wasn't sure which organ nurtured the motive. This adventure was still part mystery to him.

Joe got lost trying to find Casa Vista Oro. The first streets he found in Warm Sands seemed to twist into each other and cross back. But he wasn't worried. There was little traffic: a few pool maintenance trucks and some BMWs so far. He had found a set of touristy guesthouses, which had big signs and long parking lots. But Casa Vista Oro was probably like an estate. A more intimate setting.

Then he saw it. A well-trimmed dark green hedge covered a six-foot-tall white-washed wall that took up half the block. There was a pedestrian entrance door near the center of the wall with an elaborate call system. This door was solid wood with a small square peephole door three-quarters of the way up. The small door was covered by a metal grill, like the *mirilla* in an old Spanish convent that had allowed its residents to see out but kept the world from slipping in anything more than a love note or a cutting from a dead mother's hair.

Joe parked his car up against the wall and went over to the door. He pressed the call button. He wasn't sure how to announce himself. He was an employee now, but with a special status. He was more of an intern. Or—the reality—a sad uncle who needed a place to stay and things to do.

"It's Joe Tierney. I'm parked outside. I hope this is a good time. I'm sorry I didn't call ahead." Joe was surprised by the tone of servility in his voice. He stood back from the speaker and waited for a response. A twinge of sadness accompanied his gaze as he looked up and down the manicured street. He had been a natural leader, an ordained leader, but all that anointed authority seemed to have evaporated away with his sweat as the sun started to draw out his liquids.

He rang the buzzer again.

Then the door swung open, smooth and wide, without a creak or crack. An older gentleman with salt-and-pepper hair and a small frame stood at the entrance. They could look each other in the eyes. And his eyes were bright. And blue. A blue Joe had never seen, circled by a gray nimbus as if they hadn't yet matured. They both smiled.

"Father Joe Tierney?" asked the man with the baby-blue eyes as he stuck out his hand.

"Yes," Joe answered and straightened his spine. He had finally made contact with his future. "And Joe is fine, please." He reached out his hand, and the other man pulled him into a hug.

"Cyril Anastasis, but people call me Cy."

Cy prolonged the hug and patted Joe's back as if to strengthen the welcome. Joe let himself unwind into it. He didn't know Cy, but this embrace was exactly what his pal Edward had told him to expect. A warm, New York-Greek *amplexus* that felt both liturgical and natural.

"Thank you for helping me out," Joe said as they separated.

"Edward said so many good things about you," Cy said as he stepped back, openly appraising Joe like a casting director.

The attention made Joe start to squirm, and he found it uncomfortable to keep Cy's gaze.

"Let me show you the Casa first," Cy said. "Do you need some water? Or a restroom break?" Cy put his hand on Joe's back and directed him through the door onto a slate walkway set on one side of a large lawn, lush as a putting green. In the middle of the lawn was a lap pool that ended near a stacked stone waterfall and spa. A dozen white lounges with royal blue cushions bordered the pool, several occupied by men of Cy's age.

Joe stood still for a second to take it in, then Cy nudged him on. This guesthouse was like a sanctuary. So restful. So full of peaceful colors and the light sound of water slowly dripping down the stone. Joe kept awakening to more of the details: music in the background, a soft fusion; a series of rooms bordering the lawn with windows for walls; and rich, oiled wood encasing the windows. A covered walkway provided protection from the sun and a place to eat outside one's room. The few short and colorful hedges of bougainvillea, honeysuckle, and lantana were in bloom. Hummingbirds hovered and fed at the flowers.

Nothing obstructed the monumental view of San Jacinto's slopes sitting impassively in the day's heat.

"Let's get out of this sun, Joe. Does it sound odd that I call you just Joe? You can be honest with me." Cy said.

Joe turned and smiled. "Yes, a little. I'm not a priest now—officially—anyway." Joe's smile dimmed. That admission felt awkward, as if he wanted Cy to be his friend. Joe needed to go elsewhere in this conversation.

"Your establishment is gorgeous. And kept to perfection! It's got to take a lot of work," Joe said and winked. There, he'd used a wink, a new step forward for him. Joe's mind now focused on making a good impression. He wanted to be in this place. It made his soul relax and breathe easily.

"I'm glad to have you with us," Cy said, putting an arm on Joe's shoulder. "I'll show you around and introduce you to Luis. You've spoken to him on the phone. He is the chief custodian and can explain your duties." Cy removed his hand and turned to face Joe. "I try not to hover too much, but this place is my baby."

"I'll do my best to be careful," Joe said, with a slight head bow. His first day was going more easily than he had anticipated. He wasn't being asked to pee in a cup or to show citizenship papers, and he wasn't being thrown a mop and scrub brush.

"Everyone on the staff is important," Cy said. "We promise a relaxing and attentive environment to our guests. You'll play an important part in fulfilling that promise. I'm sure it won't be a problem for you, given your background."

Joe shrugged his shoulders and batted his eyes. What could he say? He wanted to drop the priest talk, but it also made him feel whole. Still, he had to get a new dialogue going, one that wasn't built around anointed hands and holy rites.

"I've never been known as entertaining," Joe said, deciding to do some personal revelation. "But I've worked hard all my life. At my dad's hardware store. Doing chores at home. Managing a large parish. And working with the immigrant community back home. I am ready to do whatever you need done. I'm just happy to have a place to land."

And with that, Cy seemed satisfied with Joe's tone, happy, perhaps, at the subservience. Cy picked up the pace and continued showing Joe around, emphasizing the beauty and quality of Casa Vista Oro as if

Joe were about to plunk down his black American Express card.

"So," Cy said, "that's the Casa Vista Oro. It's named after the October-morning sunrise that layers a golden, shimmering scarf ever so briefly on the mountains." Cy stopped a second, seeming to assess Joe again. "I'm sure you'll hear that patter often as people stop in to plan their next year's vacation. You may have to give it yourself."

Joe's eyes opened wide. He hadn't been paying enough attention.

"Don't worry," Cy said. "You've got a lot on your mind. It's probably hard to concentrate."

* * *

Cy had left Joe with Luis and nearly skipped as he walked away. Everything was perfect, like a well-set table, place cards thoughtfully arranged. Fr. Edward had been right about Joe. Lovely man, beautiful really. Receptive to change. A soul in need of respite. Cy was in his element. He was an agent of change in the lives of others.

And Luis seemed to have no problem with letting Joe join their cozy family of cleaners and pillow fluffers and order takers. Luis had been calm when told about Joe's situation: HIV and priesthood and an ex-boyfriend eighty miles away. Nothing that unusual for Palm Springs. Luis even grinned happily as Joe accepted an offer to let a room in Luis's apartment. Of course, the complex Luis lived in was one Cy and Matt owned. They let the rooms at a reduced rate to staff, even though friends accused Cy and Matt of sharecropping their staff, binding everyone closer to them. Cy didn't care about the critique. It was all done for love. The only thing that mattered was your motivation.

With Joe's shirt size in hand, Cy drove off to Cathedral City to get ten work shirts embroidered, seven white and three black for the times when they hosted an event. He had also pressed a few hundred dollars into Joe's pants, whispering to him to buy a dozen khaki shorts from Target. Joe's eyes popped when Cy's hand pushed into his front pocket, but Cy didn't mind. Joe needed to acclimate to the desert's gay culture where touching was allowed. Cy didn't worry, despite Joe's darting eyes. Obviously Joe was out of his element, having been so long behind the altar, almost like a statue on a stand. But Joe would adjust. He was young. His spirit was broken, yes, but it had to be supple. Otherwise, Edward would not have sent him.

* * *

Luis and Joe were alone now in the utility room. While Luis averted his eyes, Joe changed into an old pair of shorts and top, clothes Luis kept at the Casa in case he got too dirty. Luis smiled and told Joe he looked good in the gear.

Joe smiled back. Inside he fought an unexpected urge to turn and run. Maybe this transition was happening too fast. Maybe this was the wrong environment for him. Yet Luis seemed kind, with beautiful dark eyes, a look much like his own.

They soon lapsed into Spanish, and Joe learned Luis's family was from Chihuahua, which was clear in his accent, the *golpeado*, a slightly louder, aggressive sing-song tone. And Luis promised to introduce him to the best *taquerías y mercados.*

While Luis showed Joe the utility room where dishes were washed and the supplies were kept, he explained why they should stick to English, unless a guest spoke to them in Spanish. Luis told him Cy didn't want the staff to build a barrier between themselves and the guests. They were to be approachable, able to answer a guest's question or offer a few moments of banter. But for only a few moments. They weren't geishas, Luis said, then giggled.

Joe rocked on his feet, something he did when he was uncomfortable. He'd been Father Joe. Father Tierney. A man others sought out for consolation and comfort. He wasn't eye candy for wealthy gay men.

"You'll enjoy it here," Luis said, nudging Joe's shoulder with his own.

The soft nudge, the day's heat, and the narrowness of the small room set off a wave of anxiety in Joe. The sweat gathered on his forehead, and his head swiveled around like a child looking for an escape route.

Thankfully, Luis stood back, probably picking up the tension radiating through the fibers of Joe's being. "Come on. I'll show you the laundry room. We have to get two rooms ready for occupancy. You can strip the beds and wash the sheets and towels. Okay?"

Joe relaxed his shoulders and released a deep sigh. Laundry sounded normal. It's the sort of stuff he did for himself. He'd done it since he was a child helping out at home.

* * *

After Cy returned from Cathedral City, he went into his small office and threw himself into his swivel chair, spinning with happiness. He couldn't get over it. Joe was exactly what he had hoped for. Dazed. Cute. Vulnerable. Full of longing.

Cy reached for his cell and dialed Edward. He had to thank his old Episcopal pal for sending him this catch.

"Hello?" Edward answered on the third ring. "Is that you, Cy?"

"I'm here, and he's arrived. He's exactly what you said. This is the perfect place for him. I'm so excited, I could kiss a toad!"

"Whoa, cowboy," Edward said, his chortling laugh following after. "I'm glad to hear he's made it. We've been wondering how today would go."

"We?" Cy asked. "Who's we?"

"Oh...it's Joe's friend. Pascal. I'm sure you'll hear about him. I'm over at his place for coffee. He's right here."

"I see," Cy answered. He was feeling the joy huff away. He wanted to be the savior here, the new center of Joe's life. Maybe Joe had more gay friends than Cy had anticipated. "Has Joe called yet to tell you that he's in Palm Springs?"

"Not yet," Edward answered. "We were hoping to hear later. We know this is a big day for him. We hope he settles in well."

"I'll see to that," Cy said, pleased that Joe's focus was now in the gay byways of Warm Sands and not back in the cultivated vastness of the Midwest.

* * *

Pascal shifted on the patchy, weathered sofa in the living room of Casa Romero, the Catholic Worker house. He picked at a thread of an aging green throw and reflected. Since Joe had left on his pilgrimage, as Pascal deemed his friend's adventure, Pascal had been inviting Edward over for chats and analyses of their common friend's well-being. At first, he'd been angry with Edward, hot-stove angry, because Edward had made it possible for Joe to leave, a decision Pascal derided as immature and cowardly. So, early on in this drama, Edward had become an object of scorn. Edward was the scoundrel who had found Joe a place to land in deserty Southern California—and even finagled him a job! Edward had handed Joe a ready set of helpful connections. And Edward probably would've driven Joe out there except, in Pascal's opinion, he was in love with Joe and couldn't face the personal denting every time Joe brought up Kenny. Ah, the golden boy Kenny in the Golden State. How could Edward, the gray-haired man in the rust belt, compete? So Pascal also had sympathy for Edward. He'd been in that same place of dark emotional gloom when the unattainable was so unattainable. But that was long ago.

Pascal watched Edward put the phone back in his satchel. The call from California was over.

"Your friend sounded enthusiastic," Pascal said, priming the pump and waiting for more. This part was easy; Edward always spilled his gut. Maybe it was years in the Episcopal parish trade that taught him to lead by example. Be forthcoming. A good way to describe Edward.

Edward shifted, straightening the front of his ironed clerics. He'd just come from Morning Prayer, a new stab at building a stronger community for the retirees in his parish.

"Yes, Cy is always enthusiastic..." Edward paused.

Pascal thought Edward was evaluating a thought for its confidence level. Something was nibbling at his conscience.

"I hope he'll be good for Joe. For sure, Cy'll make Joe's adjustment easier," Edward finished.

"And so," Pascal said, tucking his leg deeper onto the sofa, seeming so nonchalant, "tell me why you're nervous."

Edward coughed. "Well, Cy has his ways. He's got a good heart, mind you. But it's still a human heart and, as such, has chambers for desire. And Joe is desirable, as you know."

"Does Cy know why Joe is landing in Palm Springs? Because of its proximity to the gilded idol, aka Kenny?" Pascal asked as he leaned in for the answer.

"Yes, he knows the whole story. As much as I know, anyway. But that's a tale from the past in Cy's eyes. Palm Springs is for reinvention. That's his phrase. It's a paradise in a land of live and let live. He's always saying that. So what I'm getting to is...Cy doesn't care about Kenny or HIV. Cy will care about the new scared puppy at the door."

"And he's the dog trainer? Or the alpha male?" Pascal asked, feeling his concern stoke up. Pascal squinted his eyes. "Your friend will find that Joe is no pushover."

* * *

After a couple of hours following Luis's well-mannered instructions and letting the last days of cooped-up anxiety sweat out into the guest-house air, Joe was ready to collapse. He was the balloon that popped, flew about, and now was a spent latex scrap. They had cleaned five of the eleven rooms more thoroughly than he'd ever cleaned anything. Luis's rigor impressed Joe. No wonder Luis was in great shape. He was in constant motion, with a rag tucked into his belt like a sheriff's six-shooter. Luis could drop to the floor, eradicate a scuff, and rise back up with the speed and purpose of a CrossFit instructor. Joe was seeing a whole new set of demands stack up before him.

And then there were the guests, some who nodded politely, some who ignored them as if they were a lesser species, and some who engaged. Luis knew how to deal with each type.

They had just finished delivering the lunches and could now take a rest. Joe looked at the loungers and wished he could settle into one. Just then, Luis asked if he was hungry. In an instant, Joe's mouth started to water. Luis had promised to show him the best places for real *cocina Mexicana.*

"There's a restaurant where the gardeners go when they want a break from home-cooked meals. It's down near the Tool Shed. I'll drive. Okay?" Luis said. "We can't stay long because we have to collect the lunch dishes and wash them."

The plan sounded fine to Joe. They'd have a chance to chat more. Joe could tell that Luis had been suppressing the urge to say *"Padre"* all day, being polite and formal, saying nothing too overtly sexual after that early comment about geishas. Joe assumed his story of vocational ruin had been broadcast to Luis and Samuel, the day manager, as well as the staff. His story of woe would explain why an educated and competent man suddenly appeared at the Casa Vista Oro to start a job scrubbing porcelain.

But Joe needed to become a person, not a mythology. So it would be good to chat with Luis. "Yes, let's go. I'm starving." He'd start his reinvention with Luis over rice and beans.

Tapalpa was just as Joe imagined: the welcoming smells of frying meats, onions, and peppers; the patter in Mexican Spanish; the brassy sound of KLOB from Thousand Palms. It was a room full of men nestled into booths that abutted the two walls of windows. A scattering of tables hosted a few single guys. Everyone had dark skin and wore jeans and denim shirts with the name of a gardening company stitched over the heart. Joe fit in here. He looked over at Luis, who was waving hello to the waitress, and nodded his satisfaction.

Joe ordered *Bistec a la Mexicana* and took a big gulp from the cool Corona that Lupe had brought him. She had treated him like another worker. Maybe even being a little flirtatious toward the new man; her dark eyelashes had fluttered oh so briefly. Good. He wasn't sending off the holy vibe that his buddy Pascal said flowed too eagerly after his ordination. And there must have been no rumor about his priesthood. Otherwise, all the heads in the restaurant would have turned to stare, probably full of Mexican disappointment and confusion and anger, similar to the brew of emotions he carried around in that little brass pot he called a soul.

"I think you'll like it here in Palm Springs," Luis smiled. "Working at Casa Vista Oro is mostly enjoyable. Every so often you get a real *bruja* of a queen, but Cy always knows how to deal with that type of witch."

"I'm liking it already," Joe said and paused, not sure how to open up without dumping out the whole satchel of worries and wants that had accompanied him here. He wanted to remain opaque for a while—probably his normal self, he silently surmised. The thought hovered a moment and darkened his spirit.

And then the young man walked in. The one Joe had seen at the coffee shop. Tall, lean, luxurious curly hair, moving like a person of note, a prince of this desert town. The young man had changed clothes, no longer sporting gym shorts and a tank top. But he wasn't dressed like a *labrador* or even a skilled *obrero*. He was dressed like a *gringo* with money in his pockets.

And people recognized him. The men all turned to watch him, holding their tacos and burritos still for a moment. He fascinates them, Joe thought, maybe with an image of what they wanted to be, a brown face who wears cool colors with ease and comfort.

Or maybe an image of what they hated but were too polite to reject openly. Joe didn't know what these working guys made of all the gay culture pulsing around them.

The young man nodded to the waitress at the counter, which had plenty of open spots, then turned to sit at one of the tables in the center of the dining hall. He unfolded his napkin and took out the silverware, placing the fork, knife, and spoon in the correct positions. Then he looked up and smiled at Joe.

Luis nudged Joe's feet, "You've got an admirer."

Joe kept the young man's gaze a moment, then turned to Luis, who had all at once become a confidante, and asked, "Do you know him? I saw him when I stopped for coffee on my way into town."

"He visits Casa Vista Oro every so often. He provides services to our guests, if you catch my meaning." Luis checked his watch, signaling that either this was not a leisurely meal or that he was suddenly uncomfortable.

Was Luis unsure how to treat Joe in a situation with a fizz of sexual charge? Or was he just delicate when talking about the sex trade? Joe had sat in a confessional. He knew that few people talked about sex with aplomb.

"His massage ad is in the *Desert Daily Guide* and in A4A online," Luis said, looking up from his watch and staring directly in Joe's eyes. "We let him into Casa Vista Oro because he's always respectful. And returnees request him."

"He looks young," Joe said after another glance back at the center table.

"He says he's over twenty-one. I don't know." Luis shrugged, then turned to see their meal arrive. "He's from Fresno. He's been around town for over a year.

They stopped chatting as the busy serving boy dropped off the plates. He smiled, uttering *"Buen provecho,"* and quietly disappeared.

"I don't know what to say about this...young man and his trade," Joe muttered, half to himself. "In my old job I'd reach out to him and tell him to get another career."

"I know your old job, *Padre*," Luis whispered, saying it slowly with a knowing bend of the head and a sly smile. "Let me ask, how long have you been out? Like really out. I don't want to presume, but such things, the sale of sexual services—or just touching—are a part of our culture here in Palm Springs." Luis looked down at his hands for a moment. "It is a paradise that offers more than beautiful scenery and lots of great weather. Gay men like to have fun on vacation. And so do the straights. Sex is here but subtle, more in the shade or behind high walls."

Joe stared into Luis's eyes then over at the young man. He scratched his arms. Something had made him itch. Was he a prude, just as Pascal had said? But he had to admit his attention had spiked as he watched *el hombre joven* at the center table and examined his muscled arms and smooth caramel skin.

Joe looked back at Luis, but before he could respond, the young man showed up at their booth. A silence fell onto the room. Heads turned; ears were cocked.

"I'm Oscar," said the young man, extending his hand to Joe. Oscar held Joe's hand firmly for more than a second, long enough to further unnerve Joe. "Oscar Del Rio."

"I'm Joe. Joe Tierney." He got the words out, barely remembering to leave off the "Father" and starting to sweat and fidget. His mind whipped through all sorts of thoughts and fears and innuendoes until he stopped on Jesus and the tax collector and Joe blurted out. "Will you join us?"

Oscar moved to slide in next to Joe. The young man bumped Joe's shoulder on his way in, making Joe scoot over and say "Sorry."

Oscar's left hand went down to pat Joe's right thigh. "Thank you for inviting me. It's more fun to eat with others."

Joe rolled his shoulders slightly and stared wide-eyed at their new guest. He could see just how long the eyelashes were as they briefly dipped up and down. And he couldn't take his eyes off the nicely formed chest and muscled upper arms that showed well in Oscar's polo.

The chatter within the room started to pick up but was more subdued as if all were waiting for something dramatic.

Oscar wasn't staring at their food or looking across the table at Luis. His head was still turned toward Joe, making Joe fret with anxiety, fearful of how everyone would perceive him now—from Luis and the other diners to the waitress who would tell the cooks.

Then the waitress showed up, pad in hand with an amused smile on her face.

"Please...order," Joe spat out as if it were a last-minute thought. He briefly looked down at his food, then up. "We don't have long here," he said nodding toward Luis, who had started to eat, then stopped a moment only to gaze at Joe and grace him with a wan smile.

"*Número ocho, Lupe. Como siempre,*" Oscar said, shrugging his shoulders and ordering his usual plate of enchiladas.

"You're a regular?" Joe asked, cueing off the order.

Oscar turned his head as if the question was oddly timed or childish. "I am. Lupe is from my hometown. Our families are acquainted." Then he turned to look at Luis. "Didn't Luis inform you completely about me?"

At which Luis replied, "I was about to fill our new worker in on your specifics, Oscar. But I am happy to let you explain yourself, as you know the subject best." Then Luis returned to eating, nearing the end of his tacos.

Joe decided he had to eat, even if his hunger had now disappeared in the presence of this assertive enchanter, whose hand remained on his thigh, slowly massaging it. Joe picked up his fork and managed one bite. Oscar watched him the entire time.

"You were taught well," Oscar said, a pensive shadow in his voice. "Your manners. The way you chew. The way you hold *el tenedor,* not like another greasy tool but the way a gentleman holds a fork."

Joe didn't know what to say. He looked over at Luis, who had looked up from an empty plate. Now Joe's imperturbable work companion wasn't smiling. Luis raised his left arm to look at his high-blue Swatch and shrugged his right shoulder.

Joe began to eat quickly. Never before had he left a comment like the fork one unanswered. What could he say? That he had observed his parents and learned from them? Maybe his father's hands had guided him. He didn't remember. But who observes another like this? Hadn't he observed Kenny with a curator's eyes, checking out how Kenny tied his shoelaces with that double lacing at the top or the way he held a beer bottle and scratched at the label? But he had been in love with Kenny. Still was, wasn't he?

"Please, don't let me disturb you," Oscar said, breaking the silence. The rest of the restaurant had returned to its regular hum, sensing the drama was over—the characters now swept into a Palm Springs scene of domesticity.

Joe merely nodded at Oscar and finished off the meal, ending with a final swig of the Corona.

Luis was shifting his lithe frame to leave the booth.

Joe looked at Oscar with an unabated disquiet and said, "Excuse me, Oscar. I've got to leave. I'll see you again? At Casa Vista Oro?"

Oscar moved to let Joe out but placed his hand almost in Joe's crotch as he pivoted out. "I'm sure we'll meet again. I want to know more about you."

Joe's jaw dropped. He was afire now and didn't want Luis or the restaurant crew to see him. What had become of modest Father Joe?

Joe stood up and said nothing, trying to calm himself with distracting thoughts of his next chores. He and Luis paid at the counter, saying little to each other as they walked out into the climbing heat. Joe decided not to look back at the booth, but he imagined Oscar's eyes were following their exit.

* * *

The Desert Rest apartment complex Luis lived in was small. Ten apartments near East Palm Canyon. Joe had a room to himself but would share the second-floor apartment with Luis and a cat named Rodolfo.

The furnishings were nicer than he expected. He must've arched his amazed eyebrows a bit too high because Luis explained that Cy knew plenty of people who remodeled their homes with the frequency of air filter changes. So Luis was able to get great items, usually at the reasonable expense of picking them up and hauling them away.

"It's beautiful," Joe said, tired and hoping to crash, maybe pull himself together. They had worked later than expected. It was nearly four thirty.

"Normally, we will eat our meals separately, but tonight I will cook for both of us. *Huevos revueltos,* okay?" Luis asked.

Joe knew he'd need to eat, so Luis's offer sounded better than a trek to the Carl's Jr. on Ramon. But he wanted to unpack some and rest first and, hopefully, find a place or time to reflect. No one had been at the pool when they arrived at the apartment. Maybe he could rest in the shade of an umbrella. Look at the darkening sky. Watch the mountain.

"Can you give me some time, though?" Joe asked. "I feel the need to decompress."

Luis laughed. "I know I'm an early diner. A couple of hours enough?"

"Perfect." Two hours sounded like a release from jail. Joe hurried to his room and started to unpack his suitcases and the five boxes he'd managed to stuff into his Honda. Not much, he reflected. The lack of possessions had once felt like a shield against greed and the pull of modern commercial America. Right then, Joe looked at his belongings and wondered if this was to be the sum of his life. A sum not far from zero, just the amount Pascal would have urged. But he wasn't Pascal.

And he was traveling far from that neomonastic lifestyle.

Joe sat on his bed and checked his phone. Nothing from Kenny. He hadn't heard from him in days, which made a dark ball start to form in his stomach. Sighing, he went over to his bedroom window and studied the walkway between the apartment buildings. Everything was quiet. Low lights bordered the walkway, which was now in shadow. He could make out the barrel cacti and lantana.

He decided to lay down, setting his alarm.

Dinner was simple. Luis had scrambled some eggs and layered it with homemade salsa and cut-up fresh avocado.

"Wonderful meal, Luis," Joe said as he wiped up his plate with a *trozo* of soft tortilla.

After eating, both men got a Corona and sat back down at the table. Joe tipped his bottle to Luis, acknowledging a fine meal. He inwardly thanked his host for not spicing this mealtime with questions, which made Joe willing to open up about his life.

Most of the conversation was about families. Luis had a very normal Mexican family: tight, living near each other in a village near Delicias, Chihuahua. They had small farms, growing chilies, pecans—all nourished by the Conchos River. Luis had followed an older sister *al norte* when the family determined sweet Huicho was not meant for farm labor. His sister helped him get a job cleaning offices at night. And so a career began.

Joe described his family as more traditional American. Filled with unspoken tensions. Far-flung.

Luis's oldest sister lived in Texas, where she'd gone for work before America got crazy about illegals, fifteen years before Reagan's amnesty. "Anyway, Eagle Pass is almost Mexico, sitting just across from Nogales, with a Hispanic population that rivals most Chihuahuan cities," he allowed.

Joe's only sister was in College Station, Texas, and worked as a waitress in her husband's family's restaurant, where Spanglish was spoken but English prevailed. "That's about all I know. Elena took off when I was young. My father and Elena were similar: opinionated, strong, willing to take a risk. Her risk was to pack up and head to a college town where we had an aunt. It worked out for her, I guess. She found love—or at least she married a guy. We lost contact. Or I did. Mom heard from her sister, the conduit of information. Elena managed to hook up with a Pentecostal who was serious about male governance of the home. What an irony!"

Joe suddenly felt a weight of sadness. "I haven't been much of a brother. She doesn't even know about me." He set his beer down and placed his elbows on the table, then coddled his head in his hands.

Luis said nothing; he didn't move. A buzzing tension hummed in the quiet room. And, then, Joe's phone rang in his bedroom.

Chapter 4

Joe startled from a trance he was in, where he was seeing his sister's face as he acknowledged his flaws and, now, his notoriety.

He was at the table, and his phone was ringing. He shot up from the dining room chair, nearly knocking it over, and ran to his bedroom. It was a phone call, but could it be from Kenny? On his first night in California?

He pressed the answer button. "Joe Tierney here." Joe knew he sounded breathy, maybe anxious.

"I know that voice."

It was Kenny. Joe's reaction was immediate. Hope surged in his soul. He fell onto his bed, his smile broad. Kenny had called. His first night in California! Joe hadn't been sure there'd be any contact anymore, not since he'd heard about Jasper. And given the mess between the two of them. The way they split. And now the HIV.

But a call! On his first night in Palm Springs. So Kenny was paying attention.

"Thanks for calling, Kenny." Joe heard the joy singing in his voice. "It means a lot. I arrived today. I'm off on this adventure, you know, or monumental fuckup, maybe. Wow, it's just good to hear from you."

Joe stopped a moment, realizing his gush was probably making Kenny's thumb hover on the disconnect button.

There was silence. Joe started to scratch his chin and sat up on the edge of the bed.

"I kinda know what it's like, Joe. You know, after we split up. I made my way out here to start afresh. It's been good. Was really good until…"

Joe's heart skipped a beat. He didn't want to do this on the phone.

"I know," Joe said. "It's shitty stuff, this HIV."

"I'm so sorry I got you into this," Kenny said.

Joe's chest tightened as he picked up the anguish in Kenny's voice.

"I wish there was something I could do to make it all right," Kenny added.

A thought wandered out from a dark corner of Joe's brain: *HIV is going to bring us together again.* He held the phone a little closer. "Thanks, tall guy," he said, dragging up one of his affectionate names. Joe paused, maybe that was too far. "I'd like to see you, if that's okay."

"Okay? You mean because of Jasper?"

"Jasper, yeah. And because of how we ended." Joe said.

"We ended rough. It seemed rougher on me because I didn't want to end it," Kenny said.

Joe remembered the night of the split; Kenny was stunned and had little to say, probably because Joe had become a walled city and had spent the night flinging out his reasons for ending their relationship.

"I know I hurt you," Joe said, almost whispering into the phone.

"I've talked it over with Jasper. It's okay with him if I meet with you. He's all about being up front."

Joe heard Kenny breathe in deeply, then let it out.

"And I'd like to see you again too. To apologize face-to-face. I really did you wrong, Joe." Kenny paused again. "Look, I'll be in touch about when I can come see you. And you're doing okay?"

"I look forward to hearing from you," Joe said, feeling the sadness creep back in his voice. "I'm okay here. It's good to keep my body moving. And Palm Springs seems like a decent enough place to land."

* * *

Kenny called Jasper as soon as he had hung up with Joe. It was part of their contract, the Joe clause. Jasper had said, "I want to hear from you right away." Jasper wasn't one to let problems build up and overwhelm. And he had made it clear he wanted to help map out this forgiveness campaign.

Kenny had no complaint with Jasper's involvement, his oversight. He would even let Jasper wire him with mic and camera. Why? Partially because Kenny had laid a lot on Jasper. First HIV. And now an ex-lover in town. And they had just started to get to know each other, to meld, to enjoy rubbing up to each other on a long Sunday morning.

"I'm glad you made the call," Jasper said. "And how's Joe doing?"

"He says he's okay. He sounded okay. We didn't talk much. He's settling into Warm Sands. He called it a place to land."

Kenny knew Jasper wouldn't think much of Joe's landing zone, Warm Sands. It was a set-apart area in south Palm Springs where gay men could unpack their suitcases and unlock their desires. The area had a rep. And Jasper had very strict morals, which included no partying, no playing around, and no public nudity. Jasper was a Marine officer, and he stood upright and pinned each moral standard on his chest like a medal. He was strict. But, in his way, similar to Joe.

"We didn't talk long," Kenny said. "He sounded tired. And maybe a little sad. He'd only arrived."

"Are you going to meet up?"

Of course, that was the question on Jasper's mind. Totally expected.

"We will, but we haven't set a date. He's settling in, you know. But I need to see him and apologize. I need to get this off my chest."

HIV was hounding Kenny. He had just started seeing a doctor and taking meds. Everything was good—except that it wasn't. This HIV had settled in with a gloom he didn't have words for. And so he drank.

"You're doing all right?" Jasper asked, which brightened Kenny's night. This warrior guy knew what he was going through. He had asked. He'd be there to help. Wouldn't he?

* * *

Joe's phone rang again almost immediately, giving him little time to mull over his conversation with Kenny. He grabbed for the phone and checked the caller ID. Could it be Kenny calling back?!?

When he saw who it was, a swift, unexpected sorrow flitted past. It was Edward and kind of him to call, but Joe wasn't in the mood to debrief. He hadn't fully absorbed the call with Kenny. Still, Edward was a good friend, a man who'd shown him warm kindness and loving attention, who had ministered to him. Joe couldn't ignore him. He wasn't that kind of guy.

"Hey," Joe said, not knowing what to say.

"Joe, it's Edward. I'm here with Pascal. You're on speakerphone."

Joe heard a distant "Hey" from his friend Pascal, and a lump of anxiety that centered over his heart started to dissolve.

"Did you make it okay?" Edward asked.

A question Joe could handle. With his feet on the floor, he lay back on the bed. "I made it okay. And I've had my first workday. I'm still an elementary level scrubber though."

There was laughter at the other end. That sound felt good, uncomplicated.

"And you have a place to stay?

"Yes! The guys I work for have let me stay with the supervisor of their guesthouse maintenance and housekeeping crew, Luis. He's a great man and sweet. I'm staying in a room in his apartment, with everything supplied by the guesthouse. I don't have to go scrounging for a bed!"

Joe heard Pascal yell, "Watch out for snakes."

"No snakes yet, Pascal. Maybe I've got that St. Patrick's charm!"

Pascal responded, "You're only half Irish. That Mexican part won't charm away any lurking reptiles."

Joe smiled. What a pleasure to hear Pascal's sweet, boy-chipper voice. "Good to hear your voice, Pascal. I guess you must be keeping Edward company now that I've decamped to the land of the heat lamp."

He could hear Edward chuckle. "Of course we miss you and gather to remember our friend on his pilgrimage."

There was that word, "pilgrimage." The three of them had batted it around as he took counsel on his leaving. Joe sighed because he knew his journey was no typical pilgrimage, a trek of longing and openness. His journey was more a pirate's quest, he had to admit, the searching for a treasure that had been buried but never forgotten.

* * *

Cy opened the side gate and placed his fingers to his lips. He blinked his eyes but wasn't certain the young man would see it. He always blinked when he saw someone or something he liked. And this one was so desirable.

Cy had been needing this all day, ever since that cute Joe Tierney showed up and started going through his paces with Luis. That man had an ass! And a smile! Did Joe notice how often his new patron showed up during the day? Surely Luis did. He'd say something to Luis, something about wanting to make sure the new guy was working out.

And now Cy needed some working out.

"Follow me," Cy whispered and made a head movement that meant come into the compound. Cy quickly locked the gate, then led his evening's treat, a valued regular and protégé, to an empty guest room. One of the rules of his relationship with Matt was no fondling of others or by others in the confines of their own home. Spare rooms at the Casa were neutral territory.

Cy chuckled to himself as he led the young man across the grassy lawn and around the pool to the small guest room in an odd corner at the end of the compound. This was the most isolated room, with a door that opened onto the wall of concrete fronted by tall ficus trees.

"I'm glad you had a free time in your schedule," Cy said.

"For you, I am always available," replied Oscar, deliberately avoiding reuse of the word "free," which was no surprise to Cy. He was a businessman himself.

And once their session had ended, Cy might leave the room a little messed up, certainly letting the cum stains color the white sheets, requiring a good bleaching. And lube packets would remain opened and sticky on the side tables. Luis would explain it all to Joe in the morning. It wasn't too soon for Joe to learn about his new home. Sex, the hard thought of it and sometimes the sweat-dripping reality, was definitely an economic driver in Palm Springs.

* * *

Edward and Pascal sat in silence in Edward's front room. The doors and windows stood open, and the sound of crickets and rustling maples came in on a light breeze.

"How do you think he sounded?" asked Edward as he finally stopped staring at his phone, the longing inside him made it hard for him to dissemble.

"Cheery Father Joe," said Pascal, also looking at the phone, then up at Edward's sad face. "He certainly sounded happier than you look, Edward."

Edward lifted his head and produced his best priestly smile, broad and open. In his mind, however, his thoughts had narrowed to this one awareness: he missed Joe every moment of every day.

"You know I miss him," Edward said.

"I miss him too," Pascal said. "But your 'miss' is way different, honey. Way different."

Edward shifted on the sofa, leaning in slightly toward Pascal. They'd almost had this conversation all this past week. Time to dive in headfirst. Or heart first.

"I was falling in love with him," Edward said, just above a whisper. His eyes wet, he blinked back tears. "I was falling in love with him." He reached out a hand to take Pascal's arm. "He wasn't interested in me, of course. It was a bad time to meet him...when he was just coming out as gay and HIV. If we'd met differently...and his mind is so much on Kenny. I know what that's like. There's an image that fills his brain. And it's not me."

Pascal reached over and covered Edward's hand with his right hand. "I've known since day one, Edward. It's hard to hide your attraction. It's hard for anyone."

Pascal moved a bit, and Edward pulled back slightly, freeing his hand.

"I feel for you, Edward." Pascal paused a moment and took in several calming breaths.

Edward waited for more. More than commiseration and a display of yoga technique. Pascal knew Joe as well as anyone. He wanted to hear the expert's point of view.

"Joe is like a wounded soldier in a field tent burning up with a fever. His fever is Kenny. And you're right; this obsession is a feverish hallucination totally clouding his mind." Pascal was silent for a moment. "But I don't think Kenny is going to be the ultimate healer. Part of Kenny is a mirage, a glimpse of paradise from Joe's fever cot. When the fever abates—and it will—then Joe will reevaluate."

Pascal took another sip from his warming Heineken. "That's what I believe. I believe the storyline is going to zig and zag. We're about to get another zig—a big one. So, if you want a chance to make a connection, a deeper connection I mean, then the time is coming. Because Kenny is not the right antidote to what ails Joe. Take it from me, his old seminary pal. Kenny helped cause the fever, but he won't break it."

Chapter 5

Joe stirred from a long and sleepless night. Yes, thoughts of Kenny had kept him squirming and sweating. But Oscar had crept into bed too.

What was it with that guy that caught Joe's fancy? Yeah, Oscar was sexy. But sly. A fox.

Joe blinked his eyes to make sure of the time. He had accepted Luis's offer of a ride because, after work, they would stop at Home Depot and True Value; Luis would introduce him to his contacts at both places.

Joe was learning quickly. And Luis had told him about DAP, the Desert AIDS Project. He had to check it out, see what the odds were for getting assistance. But, so far, he was still just a tourist in Palm Springs.

This week he would spend getting a rhythm going at work and with Luis. And maybe slough off this sexual energy that had amped him last night.

There was a time, not long past, when nights like this would have been fodder for his sessions with his spiritual director. They'd talk about evil spirits. Fighting against them. Keeping thoughts of the goal in mind.

Joe smiled briefly. He had goals now, but the fleshy kind that would make his staid spiritual director cringe.

* * *

Luis and Joe arrived at 6:00 a.m. on a fresh desert morning. Their charge was to make coffee and set up the continental breakfast. The guests of Casa Vista Oro were professionals and couldn't shake off the urge to wake early, check emails, check the markets, check who was online and horny. That's how Luis explained it to Joe as they hurried out of the apartment after a brief cup of coffee and a yogurt.

"We can eat at *la Casa*," Luis had said. "Don't worry; Cy is very accommodating."

Luis assigned Joe to clean up the breakfast alcove, sweep the floor, wipe off the tables, and put out the flowers that had arrived yesterday evening. Cy wanted them to be fresh, but he wasn't obsessive, so Joe heard.

"Cutting corners," said Samuel, the day manager, very quietly and with a shake of his head.

They had to have everything set out and ready for the early risers. 7:00 a.m. That's what the website professed. "We accommodate your lifestyle." It seemed to be the slogan for Casa Vista Oro.

"Let's do the small guest room next," Luis said, heading to the side closet where they stored all their cleaning stuff. "I noticed the exit gate next to it was not properly closed."

"Oh, is that how guests leave early, out to the public parking spaces? Shouldn't they lock up and put the key in the drop box?" Joe asked.

"It wasn't a guest, I'm sure," Luis said with a broad smile. "Welcome to Palm Springs."

"I don't get it."

"It was Cy. Entertaining. Or being entertained. It happens about once every couple of weeks."

"A party in a small guest room?" Joe shook his head.

"A party...in a way. Something that should happen in private. Something we won't talk about with our employer," Luis said with a stern tone.

"Okay," Joe answered, followed by a sigh. He wasn't in the mood for mysteries. He needed to get into the Zen of cleaning. Last night's call with Kenny still played in his brain. The excitement he still felt.

Kenny had called on Joe's first night in town! Joe still had a chance.

Luis and Joe walked over to the small guest room carrying only a subset of cleaning materials. Luis didn't want to disturb slumbering guests with rolling wheels on the tiles.

The room smelled of rubbing lotion, the burning of joss sticks, and a very faint hint of bleach. The covers of the bed were thrown off, and there was obvious staining on the sheets made by oils and a yellowing substance.

"Why don't you unmake the bed and take the linen to the laundry room; bring new linen too. But we'll air the room out for a while. It's not too bad. Just a massage and release," Luis said with the vaguely bored sound of a seasoned laborer instructing a new one.

Joe went about his task as Luis went into the bathroom and loudly announced that the towels needed cleaning too. That announcement arrived while Joe was scanning the small writing desk that had all the electronic plugs a modern visitor might need. On it was a card. For massage services. With the picture of a shirtless, handsome young man. Oscar. The card had oil on it. And a thumbprint.

Joe picked it up and studied it intensely as if the card held a seminal scripture text.

Joe was still holding the card in his hand when Luis returned.

"So now you know," Luis said. "You know who was working in here last night."

Joe's shoulders slumped, and he moved to sit at the foot of the bed. He had to sit. He looked again at the card. Was this Oscar's fate?

He looked up at Luis.

"It's sad," Joe finally said. "I think it's sad. He's selling himself. I suppose he has to...or thinks he has to."

Luis was quiet, letting Joe's words settle into the now dense atmosphere of the room. It was hot outside, and Luis moved to close the door.

"Palm Springs is full of guys like Oscar," Luis eventually said. "You find them everywhere with their greeting cards and their smiles for the older guys. They're in the gym, at Friday happy hours, at Sunday tea dances, in the grocery aisle, on A4A and Craigslist—or every online site that's currently popular. You hear what I'm saying? It's part of what makes up Palm Springs. Youth bartering with old age. And many young men search out older men; they find older men attractive."

"I hear. I hear," Joe replied. He looked up at Luis, who had seemed to be lecturing him. "But it's not right that a guy has to sell his body to make a living. The body is so..."

Joe trailed off, and Luis didn't pry. Joe was going to say "sacred," but hesitated at the pious word.

"Let's clean up here," Luis said, his tone sharper than normal. "Cy will be along soon. We can talk later."

"Okay," Joe said, rising from the bed, pocketing the card, and turning to strip the linen.

But he couldn't strip out the image. Oscar had been in this room. And Cy. Cy had been the old man who bartered money for intimacy with a younger man. Cy, the man who was helping Joe get a foothold on this canyon path. So Joe was part of the chain. He and Oscar were now linked. Through Cy.

It was a short walk to the laundry room, and no one else was out. The day was hot already but bearable. The sun's angle was still benign.

* * *

By noon, Joe had recovered somewhat from the Oscar revelation. The beautiful setting and hard work had dissipated some of his gloom, and Joe felt as if he'd sweated out a couple of gallons of water. He was ready for lunch. As he headed to Luis's Mazda truck, he reached into his pocket to touch the card he'd picked up that morning. Oscar's card. Joe had decided he'd contact Oscar. His heart was directing him. He needed to speak with the young man. To hear Oscar tell his story. That's all Joe had in mind.

* * *

In San Diego, Kenny hurried up with his lunch burrito, an inexpensive snack from Tacos on Wheels, a food truck he loved. Today was the day of his usual nooner meeting with Jasper. Jasper's Jeep had tinted windows, enclosing them in a darkness that afforded them cover for a quick hand job at some off-base locale. But Kenny had gotten a text from Jasper saying he couldn't make it. The text had made Kenny's stomach clench and his appetite drop to zero. Did this text foreshadow something? Was Jasper having second thoughts, now that the HIV priest was sheltering nearby?

Kenny finished the burrito and crumpled the paper wrap.

He was on base, near Del Mar, and there were tons of hot guys around. The visuals were having their normal effect. Kenny had some time to kill and didn't want to head back to today's rewiring job. He got in his F-150 and headed out on I-5 to a rest area with an overlook so he could scope out the beach and ocean, his happy places. So rousing for a Midwestern boy. The air, the colors, the gulls stirring up the shore with their frenzy. And maybe he needed some of that rousing that came with fresh air and a vista of endless possibilities, something that might release the tension he was feeling in his tight jeans.

Kenny parked his F-150. He put on his Dodger's cap, stepped outside, and bent backward, stretching his spine, the way he'd seen his dad do for what seemed like centuries. That made him smile.

A smile that was wiped away instantly when he thought about his HIV and how he could never tell his parents. His shoulders sagged with the thought as he bent forward. Slowly Kenny walked to the front of his truck and rested against the grille.

It took a while for the worrying thoughts to pass, but as he kept staring at the ocean and the empty parking lot, Kenny began to get hard again. HIV didn't stop that organ from pumping blood. Not yet. And now what? He looked around to make sure he was still alone, that no one had a spyglass on him. Jasper...that was Jasper speaking inside his head.

After he came, Kenny unwound for a few drowsy seconds. And then the flash in his hazy mind. He'd been thinking of Joe when he came. No doubt about it.

* * *

After dinner Joe excused himself and went to his bedroom, shucking off his sandals and laying propped up with his back on his pillows. He had his phone in one hand and Oscar's card in the other. Had Oscar left the card for him? Yeah, part of Joe wanted that set of facts. Joe knew Oscar was smart, calculating. Oscar hadn't left the card for Cy or Luis; Cy had his contact info and Luis didn't like him.

So, what might Oscar want from him? Advice? Affection? Companionship? Not money, he hoped.

Joe got up from the bed, flipping the card onto the duvet. Maybe he'd call later. He put on his nicer sneakers and walked out into the kitchen. Luis was out there working on a salsa for the next day. There was a Front Runners potluck at an estate in Deepwell he was going to attend, an invite from friends.

"I think I'm going out for a drink," Joe said, sounding sheepish, which made him shift on his feet. He was a grown man, after all.

"If you want a quiet place that's not high pressure, go to the Tool Shed," Luis said, looking up from his cilantro. "Yeah, it's a leather and Levi bar, but it's also a neighborhood place. Just have a beer. Chill. You have your key. I'll probably be in bed when you return."

Joe nodded, relieved Luis hadn't given him a lecture about work in the morning.

The Tool Shed was on Sunny Dunes. It was past a row of retail stores that were just past *Tapalpa.* Joe smiled. *It is a small town,* he thought.

He parked near a door into a bar with black-tinted windows and a graphic of an oversized hammer encircled by a sinuous "S." The words "Tool Shed" stood out underneath the graphic. Cute idea. The bar bordered a lumber yard. However, Joe couldn't get a read on the building. Outside seemed a little seedy, forlorn, not the sort of place Luis would frequent. Concrete and opacity. Joe shrugged, got out of the car, and headed inside anyway.

He was in shorts, t-shirt, and sneakers. He'd heard that some leather bars had dress codes. He'd soon find out. Since his was the only car parked out front, he expected the bartender would be happy for any customer, even a confused-looking walk-in.

As he pushed through the black plastic strips at the front door, his eyes adjusted quickly to the dim lights.

He saw varied scenes: a bar, benches, empty tables and chairs, a room with a pool table, and a darkened, fenced-off area. Three older guys in flip-flops were huddled in conversation at the bar. Bearded men in shorts and tees, like him, sat on one bench. Around the pool table, two men holding cues were slowly circling.

He had stood long enough for the two bartenders to look up at him with smiles. Did he look like some rube just wandering in from the hinterland? One of the bartenders was his age, short, with a nice build and stubbly beard. Joe walked up to his station.

"Could I get a Bud Light?" Luis had said they were cheap. Joe didn't care. He only wanted a beer.

"Draft or bottle?" A question. Joe had to think. The bartender was cute. His smile was worth any dental bills to keep it glowing.

"Draft." Joe reached into his front pocket for a wad of cash, which reminded him that he had to get set up with a bank. And find a doctor. Thoughts that were immediate downers.

Joe took the glass mug and shifted back, looking for a good spot to settle. His gaze took him past the bartender whose head was gently nodding at an empty spot at the bar away from other guys.

Joe grinned and moved over to the spot, sitting on the stool. He looked up at the TV, which was showing stills of hot, muscled, hairy guys posed in dark spaces. It had never been a look that appealed to Joe, but he watched anyway. Then the bartender came by to wipe the top of the counter.

"You're visiting?" he asked.

Joe smiled. "Almost," Joe said, extending his hand. "I'm Joe. Just moved here."

"Bobby," the bartender said, gripping Joe's hand with a callused grasp, then slowly easing out of it. He offered Joe another gleaming smile.

"Hey...Bobby," Joe stammered. "A friend of mine—the guy I'm rooming with—told me to come here for a nice cool beer." He turned and looked around, then back to Bobby. "He said it was an unpressured atmosphere. That's what he called it."

Bobby grinned. "Well, there's pressure here, but not the preening peacock type. It's a neighborhood bar. We even have Bingo! Whatever pressure you get is more the leather-daddy type, but nothing too wild." Bobby paused a second to wipe the bar again.

Joe caught a glimpse on the TV of a man in chains and made a face, or so he surmised, because Bobby was taken back a bit.

"Not your type of fantasy?" Bobby asked, all serious now.

"Not really," Joe said, then sighed. "What does that make me?"

"Like many guys," Bobby said, smiling again. He leaned on the counter, both hands anchoring him, as if he were giving all his attention. "I don't discriminate. Some of my best buds love a good orgy. A party with slings, Crisco, jockstraps, and butt-slapping fun. Me, I'm more of a 'night home with my guy and my dog' type of gay."

"I'm probably that myself."

"You sound tentative. Still exploring?" Bobby asked and winked.

Another patron arrived with a pal and called out "Bobby, two beers and two shots! How're they hanging?" Bobby gave a sad little nod to Joe and moved to greet his friends.

Something in Joe, a funk, maybe, or a lingering sense of awkwardness made him get up from the bar and move over to the other room, nearer the pool table and the entrance to the smoker's pit.

Joe sat on a bench and looked back over at Bobby who was now deep in conversation with the new guys, both tall and bearded and tatted, seemingly happy and relaxed. Joe closed his eyes a moment. Could that ever be him? Happy and relaxed? At ease with all this sexual stuff? Sex being part of the bend and flow, even in a light conversation?

Then he saw him. Slender, all in white to set off his brown skin. Tank top, shorts, sneakers. And the smile. He'd just come in from the far hallway. Had he been in the bathroom? He ordered a beer and sat down on another bench, peering at his cell phone. Was he here to play a game of pool? Waiting for a call?

Then the older man came in, also from the hallway. He was a little bent over but tall nonetheless. Long pants, Hawaiian shirt untucked, sandals, and socks. He put his arms around Oscar's shoulders and leaned in to kiss him on the lips. All so fluid and easy.

That movement was a shock to Joe. He stood up, the urge to interrupt pounding in him. Then he saw Oscar turn totally toward the old man, rising from the bench, hugging him, pressing his face into the old man's neck. Then Oscar was gesturing, offering to order a drink. Suddenly Joe felt exposed. He didn't want to be seen as a lurker. But what was he?

Joe thought of escape. He began to amble over to the smoking pit, turning his face from the bar, staring instead at the cutout on the wall of a Tom of Finland caricature. He opened the pit's door with deliberate care. The two guys in a tight conversation at a high-top table looked up only briefly. As expected, the room smelled of stale cigarette ash despite the constant blowing of fans. Joe took a seat at the other high-top table near the doorway so he could look back into the Tool Shed proper through plexiglass walls. Oscar and the man were both standing. Both were drinking now. Chatting. Smiling. Their arms circling each other's waist. The older man would tug at Oscar's belt every so often.

Joe wanted to close his eyes, but couldn't. He muttered to himself he shouldn't watch this, but he had to.

Finally, Oscar and the old man headed back down the hallway. Joe concluded it must lead outside. He moved to get a better look out the smoking pit's outer wall and saw the parking lot, where the cars were.

Joe quickly left the smoking pit and made his way over to Bobby, whose friends had settled down to a game of pool.

"Another draft?" Bobby asked.

"Nah, one will do me tonight," Joe answered, smiling his best. He hoped to wake up whatever charm he had left. "Can I ask a question? Maybe a nosy one?"

Bobby stepped back a second, then forward. "Depends. I'm a bartender, you know. Kinda like a priest. A secret's a secret."

Joe squelched a "Damn." He liked Bobby. He didn't want to put him off. "Oh, no, nothing like that. Just a question about the young guy who was just here. We've had some encounters. At Koffi. At lunch." Joe stopped, weighing the current state of Bobby's goodwill. The bartender was smiling and nodding.

"Oscar," Bobby said. "You wanted his name?"

"No, no, not that. We've exchanged names. I've even got his card."

"Okay," Bobby said, blinking his eyes and looking around to see if any other patrons needed him.

Joe needed to get his question out, but he wasn't sure how to formulate it. Or what he really wanted to know.

"I don't know how to ask this, but...What's his story?

Bobby raised his eyebrows.

"You like the dude?"

Joe blanched. "Let's say I'm intrigued. I wonder what's going on. Does he make a play for everyone?"

Bobby laughed quietly. "Not quite everyone. But he's on his own. He keeps busy with the massage and escort business." Bobby hesitated. "That's usually not a long-term career. Not the escorting. What he's got right now is his youth. Youth fades. You know what I mean?"

Bobby seemed to know the lay of the land well. Maybe he'd started that way too. Started what? His gay life? Joe began to feel tired from this Oscar sadness and the day's unfamiliar exertion. What more did he want to know?

"Does he have a place to stay?" Joe finally asked.

Bobby shrugged, then smiled. "He does tonight."

Joe was awake and nervous. The apartment hadn't cooled off a lot. He stripped down and stood in front of the circulating floor fan aimed at his bed. Could he survive here in this fire pit of a climate?

And what about Oscar? Did he have a duty to this young man? That question clicked on his internal furnace, making him sweat from doubt and anxiety—and, in all honesty, a glow of lust.

Joe closed his eyes and shook his head.

It was going to be another night of fitful sleep.

Chapter 6

A week had passed since Edward and Pascal had talked to Joe, and now Edward was pacing through every room of his house with a chattering heart. In the kitchen, the dining room, the living room, the bedroom, that pump of love kept playing back old memes, a year-long string of them, mainly what-ifs and if-onlys. A particularly bitter yet teary-eyed set played about the hurt he'd felt when Joe had left to travel across the country to reconnect with a past boyfriend. Joe could have settled down into a good relationship right where he was. In a relationship with an older man, yes, but a wiser man. An HIV-positive man, similar to himself. Someone who connected with his spirit in so many ways.

Tired of just pacing around and muttering, Edward was finally ready to say the words. Yes, he was ready to go public with it.

Edward was ready to admit that he was in love with Joe and had to act now.

Ever since he'd met Joe at the clandestine support group for HIV-positive clergy, Edward had been drawn into Joe's orbit. He'd hoped to maneuver closer on a getaway trip, but that had been a disaster. Joe had rebuffed Edward's advances. There was no more romance for Joe. Joe had become an anchorite again, huddling in his clerical cave. After Kenny, the emotional lights were dimming.

Edward stopped pacing and finally settled onto the sofa in the living room. Joe was not the only one who could take a leap of faith, go off in search of love.

In truth, Edward thought Joe's decision to leave wasn't the worst thing to do. His life as a Catholic priest with HIV would become more and more untenable. Joe's spirituality would be constantly questioned. Joe's sexuality would never be addressed again, except in that twisty Catholic confessional culture.

Edward chuckled. Maybe he was sketching a picture of himself. Except he was Episcopalian and welcomed by most. Open to bishop and vestry.

But love, love with intimacy, could be elusive in the age of HIV. Especially if you were HIV and aging, with time and disease whittling away at the elements of attraction.

He would call Cy. But he didn't want to seem to pry. He didn't want to look desperate. He only wanted information.

So Edward made the call to Cy.

"Hello, Edward? Good evening to you. How are you?" Cy's tone was happy yet cautious. Cy had to know. Didn't this call make it obvious? Cy had to suspect that Edward couldn't control his interest in Joe.

"All is good here. Looking forward to a brief summer trip down the river. Pascal is going with me."

"Oooh," Cy said, drawing out this single vowel. "Are you and this Pascal seeing each other?"

Edward shut his eyes as he wondered how to turn off Cy's constant interest in matchmaking. "We're friends. In the same business, you know. Jesus work. And he offers delightful companionship."

"I think that's what you said about Joe too," Cy said, leaving his comment hanging with its barbed hook.

Edward almost disconnected but remembered how generous Cy had been in giving Joe a job and arranging a place for Joe to live. It was an act of mercy, although proffered after a picture of Joe was sent along with his résumé. Even so, Edward now felt in Cy's debt.

"Speaking of whom," Edward said, plunging down the thorny trail, "how is Joe doing? We haven't heard from him for a week."

Did that sound needy? Jeesh. Edward waited.

Cy's response was not immediate, which was so unlike the seasoned conversationalist.

"He's doing well, Edward. His job isn't challenging the way his old one was, which you would know. But I have no complaints. He's living with Luis, the man who is in charge of our guest housekeeping."

So, no real information. Or did Cy know something else? Cy always knew something else.

"I'm glad to hear he's getting into the swing of things. It's so good of you to help him out." Another thank you. It was something Edward knew to do in his trade as priest and rector.

After a second, without analyzing his words, Edward let out his real question. "And has Kenny shown up to say hello?"

Cy hesitated again. "Ah, the golden boy from the heartland. We have not seen him. Luis tells me there have been a couple of phone calls."

Edward waited for Cy to go on.

"The boy is coming though," Cy continued. "That's the plan. Kenny will come to visit. It's not a long drive from San Diego, you know. Two hours, depending on traffic. It's always 'depending on traffic' when we discuss cities beyond the San Gorgonio Pass. Nothing like our sweet village traffic." Cy changed the subject. "So, when are you coming to visit us again?"

Edward should have been ready for that question. A fair one. He hadn't been to Palm Springs in a decade. So much had changed for him. He'd settled into being divorced from his wife. He'd found an even emotional ground for his HIV. And he was older. Everything felt flatter.

"I'm thinking about it. I will, for sure. I don't want to cramp Joe's acclimation."

That sounded awkward. Acclimation? Who says that? Scientists? Edward wiped his hand over his now sweaty forehead. Why had he called? He only wanted to hear Joe's voice.

He decided to push forward. "Is Joe there now?" Edward asked.

"It's midday here. He's probably at lunch," Cy said, plainly not interested in facilitating a conversation with his new employee. "Come out and visit," Cy added, "and you can speak with him all you want—when he's not working. Speaking of which, I've got to go now. Thanks for the call, bye-bye."

And the conversation was over. Edward put his phone on the kitchen counter and stared at the birdfeeder outside. Had a cardinal just flown away? Edward sighed. What soul had been visiting him? His shoulders slumped. Lost and departed souls seemed to take up too much of his time these days. He needed something to boost him. Some good news. Someone's kind touch. Someone's careful awareness.

* * *

Oscar stretched his arms and shoulders, interlacing his hands as they met behind his back and flexing his chest as he rose from the hotel bed. The older man was asleep, totally comfortable in the presence of an unknown rent boy. Usually, his first-time clients were more suspicious, but this guy had snorted thirty milligrams of cocaine and was soon on a roller coaster of activity and troubled sleep. He had crashed during the act, his eyes shutting slowly and his arms going limp. Oscar was able to pop a load peacefully, then sleep mostly undisturbed. The guy had gotten up and wandered about the hotel suite every so often, checking out the window—but he didn't touch Oscar again. When Oscar woke, the guy was sleeping fitfully. Oscar left the stain on the sheets, proof that he deserved his pay. But he didn't think he'd meet up with this guy again. All Oscar could see was a man on a downward, destructive spiral.

Oscar rarely used drugs. It was a part of his style, his rigor. Drugs depleted him, and he hated that feeling. He thought of his drug policy as he strode over to pick up his clothing from the table near the hotel door. Oscar was a student of his own interior being and avoided all the easy road trips to nirvana because they always ended with a crumpled vehicle piled in a junkyard. That was part of what ruined his family. Drugs, alcohol—and Jesus, of course. Jesus turned into the prison warden and daily scold.

When his regularly soused mother burrowed into her Pentecostal den of recovery in Fresno, life changed for Oscar. He got meals on time, yes, but there were comments about his gait and his gaze. "Why are you staring at that man, *mijo*?" "Why are you hanging out with those *maricones, mijo*?" Which became the *No seas obvio; se nota a leguas* (Don't be obvious; you can be seen for a mile) that he heard in his keen adolescent ears as "Don't embarrass me in front of my church friends." Which soon led to visits to the pastor, pamphlets to read, DVDs to view, and finally a trip at seventeen to a "Journey to Jesus" camp that would set him "straight" but where he was nearly raped by a camp counselor, a fat man with two kids who "assisted" at degaying retreats because Jesus told him to. Yeah, freak.

He sat on the side chair to pull on his socks, thinking *That's what changed me. The revolt. So unexpected for a relatively pliant youth.*

It had been bedtime at camp, and Oscar slept in the nude. The fat man came in and silently stripped. Oscar didn't know what was going on. He froze. Then the man approached, lunged for him and flipped him over, pinning Oscar down on his bed. Oscar had never felt the force of such weight before. Soon Oscar's face was in his pillow. The man held both Oscar's hands and used a knee to jam apart his legs. Oscar had no experience of this. He'd never done anal. He didn't want to. Not with this *culo gordo* fat ass. Oscar squirmed, but the guy had said he would drug him and do it anyway. He had the drug in a Coke he'd brought with him. What a mess! *Puto culo!*

Oscar stopped struggling, and the scene changed. The guy relaxed his grip on Oscar's arms and moved one arm to stroke his own cock.

Oscar said, "Let me turn over. I want to see you."

The man waited a second. He stopped fumbling with his stuff. "Why?"

"It's my first time. I hear it's easier, better."

"Yeah, it can be, especially with your bubble butt," the guy said, chuckling like the freak he was. "But don't try anything."

He let up on Oscar and moved off him. Sadly for the man, he had no idea how nimble Oscar was or how strong were his teenage arms and what hatred was boiling inside. Oscar slammed his knuckles into the guy's throat so hard he thought he'd broken something. Then he shoved him off the bed and headed to the door, first rummaging through the man's pants. Oscar placed his hand on the door handle but did not open it.

Oscar was in charge now.

"You're going to get up and leave now, but your car keys and this baby Mace spray gun stay with me. You'll get them back when I'm ready. One mistake, and I spray you and scream. With that Coke can and me naked and the bruises on my arms, you'll be toast. Understood?"

The man had his hands at his throat, but he was breathing, a raspy breath. The fat fuck was probably sorry he'd told everybody he always carried a fresh canister of Mace. There was hatred in his eyes, and Oscar was afraid he'd have to use the Mace and scream.

The man was moving slowly, but putting on his clothes. Oscar hoped that the Coke was laced and that the oaf didn't spill it. That cocktail would be damning evidence. Nonetheless, this stunt of Oscar's was a risk. This camp was full of lunatics.

But the man seemed beaten. Fear peered out from his eyes. He slowly reached for his shoes and tugged them on. Once the guy had his shoes on, Oscar opened the door for him, hiding behind it to shield himself from wandering eyes, steadily pointing the Mace at the man's face. The hallway sounded deserted. It was late. Early morning, actually.

"I'll be back for my keys," the guy said as he left. Oscar shut the door tight and locked it. Then he quickly dressed and started to pack. The old campground was not a prison. But Oscar had come to this place against his will, so he'd been thinking of escape strategies every day. He'd already scoped out the window for an escape, unhinging the screen from the outside and wedging matchbooks he'd taken from the chapel's "burn your sins" corner along the screen's sides.

He shoved his satchel out the window, pulled himself up, and set off toward the weedy parking lot. Anger, fear, and exhilaration swirled inside him. He was on his own. He needed to survive.

Oscar remembered there was a well-traveled road twenty miles away. A road where he could hitch. He left the counselor's car on the side of the road, placing the keys under the seat because he wasn't a monster. Then he started jogging slowly, then hitching. He hitched to his cousin's in Fresno, thanks to a horny semi driver and his own sweet, youthful looks. He wouldn't return home. He'd stay with his cousin until he graduated from community college. Then he'd save enough money to get to Palm Springs. In that gay city, he'd build a life, his own life.

He'd have to harden himself. He would endure pain and hunger. But anger over tears.

* * *

Joe began to sweat as he drove to the Desert AIDS Project. It was hot, and he was nervous. Cy and Luis had convinced him to check out the organization for care.

"They have doctors, a Walgreens, case managers. Everything you need," Cy explained. "I can make a call if you want. We're major donors."

Joe didn't want that. He hated this whole scenario. This HIV thing and where it had brought him. He needed to manage it. He needed to manage it and he needed to manage himself. So far, it seemed, he had only done one. He was addressing his health care needs. But, as for Joe Tierney the person, he was coasting—barely. His spirit of hope at the new job had been washed away with Clorox and Windex. His hands smelled of chemicals. The reflective part of him wondered if his spirit was fraying from a routine that required few interactions and fewer decisions. And, adding to that dismal reflection, he hadn't touched himself since his arrival. It was weird having Luis down the hall. Weirder than his life in the rectory. He didn't know why.

And he hadn't heard again from Kenny.

Joe parked in a big lot beyond the building. As he walked toward the modern block structure, he saw a smaller lot with parking spaces for clients. Maybe he'd be one soon he thought and sighed. As he walked toward the meager shade of the building, he saw the shape of the young man he could no longer forget. He was sauntering up a walkway between, what looked like, apartments. Joe stopped a moment. He had learned that those buildings were supposed to be housing for

Desert AIDS Project clients. People who had no other choice. Was Oscar living here?

All of a sudden, another man walked past Oscar, nodding at him but moving on toward DAP. The new man stared at Joe, who had stopped ten feet from the DAP door. Then he smiled, his hollowed cheeks crinkling. The man hesitated a few feet from Joe, then continued to the door.

Joe expected he must have an appointment. As the man was going in, Joe looked back up the path for Oscar, but he had disappeared. So Joe slowly followed the smiling man into the building, although what he wanted was to hurry down that walkway to grab hold of Oscar and ask what was going on.

* * *

"I'm driving over next weekend, getting up early. I'll have lunch, then scoot back. Any longer would seem to imply something else," Kenny explained to Jasper that night, laying out what he saw as ground rules.

They were on the sofa, finishing up an evening's binge of *The Sopranos*. A bowl of popcorn sat in Jasper's lap. Jasper liked to control the food source—and he liked it when Kenny reached over toward his crotch. Kenny was leaning on Jasper's shoulder. He was waiting for the big man to say something about this trip.

Nothing. If he hadn't been leaning on one of Jasper's massive delts and feeling its warmth through his t-shirt, Kenny would have said he was getting the cold shoulder.

"I'll just pop over. Early lunch. Maybe Sherman's for some pancakes. I don't know. Meet at the restaurant. Something casual. We eat, I apologize, then go our own way."

Jasper stared at the credits on the screen.

Kenny hoped Jasper found this meet-up plan tolerable. Kenny had sensed a definite change in their relationship since Joe had appeared. Before the phone calls, the HIV, and now his arrival, Joe was just the ex. He could be put on a shelf with a smiling mug shot. That's all. Now he was here in Southern California. Even Jasper could feel his heat. Somehow Joe's presence was inflammatory, like those crazy wildfires, like the devil sparks shimmying across the landscape.

Jasper pulled away, turning at the same time to face Kenny who had to pull back after losing his perch. "You do what you have to do, Ken boy. I know you want to do this."

Kenny startled. Did he want to do this? He felt constrained, pulled into doing this because...because he had a bond with Joe. What was Jasper saying?

"It wouldn't be right to leave him out there without checking in," Kenny answered. "He's come all this way. You know he's gotta be in pain."

"I'm not feeling so good about it myself," Jasper said, leveling his head. "But I understand your sense of duty. I'm just not sure that's all it is." Jasper's eyes had taken on the Lieutenant Wylands cool gaze.

Jasper's worry, phrased perfectly, chilled Kenny. Was Kenny going to go to Palm Springs to check out the renewed Joe Tierney? The guy who was free of the cloth? The guy who was now openly gay?

Kenny looked away. He stood, turning to look down at Jasper. "You've got to trust me on this. I'm with you."

Each was silent for a few seconds. Then Kenny reached out his hand and said, "Let's hit the sack."

Slowly, without comment, Jasper got up and wrapped his arms around Kenny, making him feel as if everything might yet be okay.

Chapter 7

Joe blew out his breath. The sound of it rattled him. He hadn't realized he'd been holding it in. Was this a new thing for him?

He and Luis were home from work but the sun was still bright. He was standing, looking out the window at the walkway and the sun-bathed pool beneath them. It was nearing dinner time for the many retirees in the Coachella Valley. He smiled, thinking how he'd managed to broaden his geographical sense in these few short days. He now lived in a valley, not in a river city that stretched unstoppably into the plains.

Enough of just thinking! He needed to do it. Sure, it would make life more complicated, but the thought of it was dragging on him. Every hour. And last night in his dream... He had to call Oscar. Merely to talk. To find out about the guy.

Joe checked his watch. Luis was still working in the kitchen. It was Taco Tuesday, and Luis liked them *así así*. He was doing his prep work before having a cocktail by the pool and chatting with neighbors or journaling his thoughts in a notebook.

Joe picked up the card from his side table. It was easy to find. He had so few possessions here in the desert, nothing to clutter a surface. The card was next to his case manager's card from DAP. That sweet man was going to look into Joe's health care needs. He didn't seem surprised by Joe's aimless wandering into the desert without having his health care planned out. It happened all the time here in Palm Springs.

And why had Joe seen Oscar walking about in what he now knew for sure was subsidized housing for DAP clients? The thought, the dark thought of disease, saddened his heart. He didn't want the young man to have it. Maybe he was visiting a friend.

One more deep breath, something supposedly relaxing, then he'd call. He held the phone in his hand. It was steady and not shaking. He'd always had a steady hand holding the chalice, the host. The thought made him think about his heart.

So he called.

"Hello? Is this Oscar?" Oscar had said nothing, probably not recognizing the number or maybe waiting in case this was a crank call.

"Yes, and I recognize your voice. Joe, the hot man at Vista Oro."

Joe blushed. This wasn't what he wanted. He was pretty sure of that.

"You honor me, Oscar. I'm just a man." Joe let a beat pass, but not long enough to lose control of the conversation. "I found your card at the Casa and was thinking that I would like to get to know you, more about you."

Wow, was that a clunker of an intro?

"You mean you want to go out for coffee, like friends?"

"That's pretty much it. I need a friend here." Ouch! Sounding so sad. No reply.

"I'm assuming you work during the day," Oscar finally said, as if he had been considering a scheduling difficulty or, maybe, had some uneasiness about this appointment. "Late afternoon is good before the coffee shops close. I'm rarely busy then. Name a day. I'd like to meet with you. That's why I left the card."

Joe grinned and his dark eyes began to sparkle. "Tomorrow okay?" Joe asked. He was ready to move on this.

And, of course, he'd have to tell Luis, who would tell Cy. There was no stopping the story, whatever shape it took.

* * *

It was ten in the morning, and the sun was already blasting heat.

A great morning for the guys around the pool. A tough morning for workers, presaging an even tougher afternoon. But work for Luis and Joe was done early, around three, when the summer was at its worst. They could go home and dip into the shaded part of their complex's pool. It was one of the pleasures of Palm Springs that Joe was enjoying. Others from the complex, for the most part gay retirees or accepting straight women, might be there chatting, welcoming the young men with lively banter.

Joe wiped his brow as he bent over the utility room's sink. He'd washed and stacked the dishes and was working on scrubbing the sink. His concentration, mainly on the upcoming meet-up with Oscar, was interrupted by Luis, who entered quiet as a cat.

"Cy would like to speak with you," Luis said, his face unusually void of its normal happy contour.

Joe quickly wiped down his face with a wet paper towel and cleaned off his hands. He picked up his hat and walked over to Cy's office. It felt a little like seminary days and being called into the rector's office because he'd been out too late the night before. But Joe had mostly been an anchorite here in Palm Springs. The only contact was Luis. And Oscar. Was that it, the contact with Oscar? He started to feel his stomach churn.

Joe stood in front of Cy who remained seated at his desk. He took off his straw hat and held it in his hands in front of him. He was the image of a *peón* before the master: dark-skinned, sweaty, and subservient.

"Please, Joe, lock the door. I'd like to say something in private."

Joe's eyes narrowed and his chest tightened. He had been in work mode, a kind of meditative quiet. He wasn't ready for serious talk.

He turned slowly and moved toward the door. He half considered walking out and leaving Casa Vista Oro. He'd already found Roy's Center, a place where he could sleep. He'd seen Well in the Desert vans driving about, stopping to assist the worst off in Sunrise Park. There were ways to survive.

But he didn't walk out. He would hear this "private" matter. He turned the door's bolt ever so quietly. Maybe he'd even be pastoral.

Cy did not speak until Joe returned to the desk. "I hear you've had several encounters with Oscar, a fine young man I, and a number of our guests, sometimes employ."

Joe rocked on his feet and kept quiet.

Cy shifted in his chair and placed his elbows on the desk. He squinted at Joe in irritation. "I care about Oscar and about his safety. And I'm concerned about your HIV status and what that might mean for Oscar. Do you understand?" Cy's voice was sharp, accusatory—a tone Joe had heard from some of his less charitable parishioners when he'd come out.

Joe fiddled with his hat, mindlessly turning it like a wheel. "I'm not sure I do understand," Joe said.

"I'll be frank. I've lived through the worst of the epidemic, but it's still here—as you know. And some people continue to be careless, callous even, not willing to disclose their status. You seem to me to be one of those who is wound tight, who would find it difficult to disclose."

Joe didn't reply. He had begun to sweat.

"Sorry for being so blunt," Cy finally said. He shrugged and leaned back in the swivel chair.

Joe couldn't stop himself from nervously biting his lip. He still said nothing.

The silence made neither of them comfortable. The morning's charm had blown away over the high walls and their flowering hedges.

Finally, Joe was ready to respond. He had sworn up a storm inside but forced himself to use the most calming language he could fashion. He'd never had a conversation like this before.

"I have no intention of having sex, protected or unprotected, with Oscar. I want to know him as a friend."

That assertion was, in the main, true.

Cy nodded his head and leaned forward.

"Have you thought of a tattoo?"

Joe took a step back. What was this? He shook his head.

"You know," Cy said, smiling slightly, "one of those tattoos that declare to all the world that you're positive. A plus sign. A hazardous waste sign. Even the letters HIV. I've seen them all. It allows one to avoid the...the awkward disclosure conversation." Cy settled back in his chair, seeming content now.

Joe couldn't make sense of Cy's advice. Should he have thought of this tattoo thing himself? Was it a reality of life in the gay community, the best way to get it out there? Was Cy helping him become a little less innocent, his attempt at kindness? Any anger he'd felt at Cy's intrusion in his personal life was now sucked down a drain that emptied directly into his heart. He felt the dark HIV spirit, nourished by his insecurities, seep in to replace it. He just wanted to get out of the office.

"Thanks for the idea," Joe said. "We're done?"

Cy nodded. "You can get back to work. You're doing a great job. We're glad to have you here."

Cy's smile froze. Joe looked down at his hat, looked up briefly, nodded, turned, and left.

Cy had ruined Joe's good day. But he had acted out of concern. No? And maybe Joe was just inept at this. At this being gay and this HIV thing.

Joe didn't feel like talking until he and Luis settled in for a late lunch at *Tapalpa*. His appetite was slowly returning. And his need to talk.

But was Luis the guy to talk to?

After a mostly silent lunch, Joe decided to lay it out there. He couldn't take the tension any longer.

"So, about Cy summoning me into his office..."

Luis shifted. "You don't have to talk to me about what Cy said unless you want to."

"I have a concern. That's why I'm bringing it up."

Luis sat back a bit, straightening his spine. He nodded.

"Did you tell Cy about my contacts with Oscar?"

Luis's face darkened. Joe glanced around; it seemed to him that the whole restaurant had its ears open.

Then Luis leaned in, placing his forearms on the table. "You have to understand. I am an employee in a small, very small business. And I depend on this job...for income and for housing. So, when Cy asks me how you are adjusting, what you are doing, I tell him. I am afraid not to tell him."

With that, Luis opened and closed his hands, which Joe had learned meant that Luis had said what he was going to say.

But then Luis continued. "I'm sorry if this has caused you a problem," Luis said. "I wasn't that concerned because Cy is a major contributor to your welfare. I thought he had a right to know. And would naturally be curious."

Now Joe was nodding his head. All this made sense, this "entitlement" that Cy had. But it was starting to feel like a chain around his ankles.

Joe shuffled about in his seat, trying to stifle his irritation, which had not completely dissipated in the frankness of Luis's words. "I appreciate your honesty, Luis. And you explained the situation very well. We are both *peones* and Cy is the *patrón*."

Luis settled back on the banquette. "He is not a bad *patrón*. Not really. I have heard stories that would make you cry. People abused. Have you not?"

Joe pursed his lips because, like any *Latino* with ears, he had heard of the beatings and rapes, the cheating and the lying. Everyone had heard it. That didn't happen at Casa Vista Oro. But Cy's intervention still felt like a violation. And Luis didn't know about the tattoo suggestion. Should he tell him? Who could he tell? It humiliated him. Maybe he could tell Edward.

They sat in silence for a while. Joe looked around again to see if they were being observed. Was he getting paranoid now?

Luis looked at his watch. They had to finish the last of the cleaning in the few more hours before the heat became unbearable. Both of them rose, and Joe was left with turmoil roiling his guts. How was this supposed to be the land of renewal? The Promised Land? Everything around him seemed rotten now. Rotten, putrid, and uninteresting. Even the thought of Oscar. Or the coming meet-up with Kenny.

Joe drove to Koffi, heading out about ten minutes before his meeting with Oscar. That left him time to get a drink and secure a sequestered spot outside under a small shade tree on the south side of the great lawn. He guessed there would be fewer people there at that hour.

Joe wasn't ready to give up confessional-quality privacy quite yet, not if the conversation got personal.

Joe texted Oscar telling him of his whereabouts. Joe had been quick to put Oscar in his contact list after he'd picked up Oscar's card in the guest room. He was looking at his phone when he heard a soft voice speak his name. He turned to his right, and there was Oscar, coffee in hand and bending over toward Joe's ear.

Joe's face brightened. He thought there was something honeyed about Oscar this late afternoon, and his eyes steadied to take it all in.

Joe patted the seat of the chair next to him, saying, "Sit, sit. I hope you don't mind being outside. I thought it would be more private."

"This is fine, Joe, but only because there's a breeze," Oscar said, then paused, wrinkling his eyes. "Do you not want to be seen with me?"

Joe wiggled in his seat, extending his legs. "No, no, I'm not ashamed to be seen with you," Joe blurted out, hating to start on a bad footing. "It's for privacy," he said, gesturing around at the empty space.

"I appreciate privacy, Joe," Oscar said as he patted Joe's shoulder and shifted the second chair aslant to Joe's, making sure it was in the shade. "I also have nothing to be ashamed of. And Koffi isn't the place to exchange truly intimate facts."

Joe hung his head slightly, then looked up into Oscar's smiling face.

"Really, this is fine. I like it out here. We won't be interrupted," Oscar said, probably trying to make Joe feel better.

Joe smiled back. "Good." He cupped his coffee, then took a sip. "I don't know where to start. I have so many questions. Stupid, huh?"

Oscar patted Joe's knee. "Tell me why you came to Palm Springs, if you will."

Joe gulped the desert air and felt a hot current of emotion form within. He began to tap his feet; he had wanted to talk about Oscar. To get his mind off himself. But Oscar had taken charge, and Joe's answer came easily. He'd been working on it for weeks.

"I came here hoping to find love, maybe renew an old love. I came because I'd screwed up back home and felt the need to start over. I came to live as a gay man without people looking at me and judging me."

Oscar laughed at that, a warm laugh. Did it mean Joe sounded foolish? "It's something we all seek, the contentment of being just ourselves," Oscar quickly added. "I certainly appreciate that motivation. And looking for love." He paused, and his face became solemn. "But tell me about what happened back home."

There it was. The hot potato question. And nowhere to toss it if he was going to get to know this young man.

Joe looked down at his feet and briefly studied his shoelaces, which looked dirty and ratty, kind of like his life.

"I screwed up, like I said," Joe started, looking back at Oscar. "I had unsafe sex and am paying the price. I've got it. HIV. And back home, I didn't know what to do. I was scared, nervous, angry, depressed. You know I'm a priest?" Joe asked, having to get this fact into the mix.

Oscar shunted his head back and forth. "I thought you'd been some sort of clergy, but I didn't know. You do give off the super-kind minister vibe—with a dash of judgment."

Then Oscar smiled, which calmed Joe somewhat as he continued.

"You know, there had been this article about 'AIDS in the Priesthood' about the number of priests who'd died of AIDS and how the Church had tried to cover it up. Turns out I became a local poster boy for that article. The article caused some people to question every priest. Some bishops were vowing an active witch hunt. It was even getting into our diocese, which was pretty laid back about conservative dogma and more concentrated on service to the poor. But I got emotionally caught up in it and came out during a service at my parish. Came out as gay and as HIV."

Joe paused a moment, thinking he'd gotten the gist of it spun out. "That's pretty much why I'm here. That and Kenny. Kenny is my ex, if a closeted priest can call anyone an ex. He lives in San Diego now, near his new boyfriend."

Even Joe heard the tone of sadness in his voice as he spoke the last part of his tale. At least there was a breeze to whisk away the sweat that was flowing out of him.

Oscar was nodding. He had placed his right hand on Joe's left knee. He appeared cool and composed in the shade. "And how did you get the job at Vista Oro?"

"Oh, yeah. I forgot one of the other major parts of the story—Edward, an Episcopal priest I met in a support group for positive clergy. We became good friends. And he's a friend of Cy's."

Joe noted Oscar had lifted an eyebrow at that last bit of information.

A group of older guys, trim and fit, had gathered under a tree near them and were talking about their hike in the Whitewater Preserve early that morning, before the heat got up. Joe and Oscar listened for a bit. They seemed a happy crowd, joking and planning next week's hike up at the Tram. Joe could envision himself becoming friends with these guys.

Joe and Oscar remained quiet in the oasis of the well-watered lawn. Relaxed. Listening to the group and gazing at each other.

Joe was amazed at how peaceful he now felt. He smiled at Oscar, who was not the flip young man Joe had expected. Rather, he was easy to be with. Maybe even serene during Joe's confessional ramble. Was this gentleness the effect of Joe's story? The knowledge of his priesthood? Someday he might ask, but not today.

"So," Joe said, not sure how to pose his question, "you know Cy too."

Oscar blinked, somewhat startled. "I don't want to talk about Cy," Oscar said, sitting up a little straighter. "He's a client. A client and a special friend." Oscar's tone was sharp, defensive, almost angry.

Joe passed a hand through his hair. "I'm sorry. I'm only hoping to get to know you better. I'm not here to interrogate you."

The word "interrogate" seemed to unsettle Oscar, who shifted slightly and straightened his top. Joe, the counselor, knew they were now close to Oscar's trove of unresolved issues. Cy had to be one of them.

They sat again in silence, now an unnerving quiet that seemed to stretch. Joe studied Oscar's face, watching him gain control of that turmoil.

"I'm very careful," Oscar finally said, wading into the silence with a reflective voice. "I feel as if I'm the fighter in the ring, all day long, always needing to get my punch in or avoid someone else's jab. I don't want to burden you with that. It's not how I am, a complainer. I am a fighter and, so far, undefeated. I take care of myself."

Joe was nodding, appreciating this honest, clean statement. His smile broadened, and Oscar returned the smile.

"I don't want to take on your burden, Oscar. But I would be willing to talk about what it's like carrying it. Could we do that for each other?"

Oscar scrunched his lips as if he were considering an important choice. "Okay, let's try."

"Good," Joe said and placed a hand on Oscar's knee, hoping to seal their contract.

Oscar looked down at Joe's hand and raised an eyebrow, making Joe withdraw his hand immediately.

"Sorry about that," Joe said. "I shouldn't have touched you."

Oscar was grinning. "Usually that means I've got another client, but I know you couldn't afford me."

Joe laughed. "You're right about that. I'm a low-wage earner. Extremely low-wage. Thank God, housing is part of the deal."

"You're lucky there," Oscar said, sounding wistful. "I don't have a regular place to stay. It depends on my arrangements. And on the seasons. I've met a couple of Canadians who enjoy the company of a *Latino* boy during their stay. That's good for me. But then the summer comes and I need to find different lodging." Oscar shrugged, acknowledging the challenge. "That's when people like Cy will sometimes help. I hate going to Roy's Center. It's so sterile. And far away! No clients there!"

Joe knew Oscar was making a joke now, but he heard the desperation behind it. At least one part of his seminary training still functioned—an attentiveness to the sound of pain.

CHAPTER 8

Edward was online scouring ads. VRBO. Craigslist. He was going to spend a month in Palm Springs and needed to find a rental. He was going to follow his heart, which had been captured by Joe Tierney and dragged off into the desert. Edward had gotten the okay from the bishop and his vestry. His pal Fr. Todd Standhome from St. Paul's in Seattle was looking for a place near his ailing parents, so he could take over Edward's duties for a month and maybe help out longer if Edward's plans changed. Luckily, Edward had saved a lot over the years. With that nest egg and money he had inherited, he would be fine. Things were coming together. Maybe in another month.

But how would Joe take it? They had joked, only so briefly, before Joe left that Edward might visit him for some sun. That was back in the days when all attention was on getting Joe over the hump of diagnosis and despair. Now Edward had chosen to hop on a plane in the chance that Palm Springs Joe might view their relationship differently.

First, find a place. No way could he afford to stay at Casa Vista Oro for a month, even if it was out of season. He'd have to have a Hollywood salary for that expense!

He needed only one or two bedrooms—furnished, of course. Something in central Palm Springs would be nice so he could walk downtown, or something in the southern part of the city near shopping. He'd rent a car. He was getting excited.

* * *

Kenny was going to give Joe a call and finalize their meeting place and time. It was eight o'clock, not too late to call. He and Jasper had taken in a movie and burgers at Urban Mo's in Hillcrest. They liked the energy there, even if it got a bit crowded for Jasper's tastes. Jasper liked his men quiet and lined up in rows. That's how Kenny joked about Jasper's tastes—humor that usually went over pretty well with the big guy, rewarding Kenny with a smile and, maybe, a grab from those muscled arms.

Planning the rendezvous with Joe, Kenny thought about what he was going to say. Where to meet, that was top. And what time to meet.

Such an easy call to assure their plan was clear, but so hard to punch in the numbers. On this cool evening, Kenny was sweating. He finally sat down at the kitchen table, waited another minute, then picked up the phone.

One ring. Two. Three. Maybe message time.

"Hello...Kenny?"

Joe's voice was breathy but upbeat.

"Hey, Joe. You had to run to get your phone?"

Joe laughed. "Yeah, I was in the pool, luckily at the shallow end. But I made it. I was expecting a call. Are we still on for tomorrow?"

"Definitely, dude. Tomorrow around noon. Sherman's Deli on Tahquitz. You know the place? Great breakfast food. Just like back home. I'll be ready for a helping of pancakes."

"I know where it is. You can get syrup in your mustache and lick it for hours!"

Aargh! Kenny wanted to smile but winced instead. Joe can't be bringing up memories. Not like they were two old lovers contented with each other as they flipped through an album.

"I'm clean-shaven now. Marine style. You'll see."

Joe was silent, then he said, "I look forward to seeing you."

Kenny closed his eyes. There was so much going on here. So much that made Kenny ill at ease. But he needed to meet with Joe. "You'll know what to do" is what Jasper had said. The thought of Jasper made

Kenny sit up in his chair.

"Okay, then," Kenny said, not responding directly to Joe's comment. "I'll see you tomorrow. Enjoy your time in the pool." Silence again. Joe must have been expecting a longer conversation.

"Yeah, I'll get a few laps in," Joe finally said. "See you tomorrow."

Joe looked up at the sky and saw a threatening row of dark clouds begin to roll in. He wondered if their presence meant anything.

* * *

Edward asked Pascal over that night for dinner. He'd found a new brussels sprout dish that cooked in the broiler. He wanted Pascal's opinion.

And Edward wanted to confess.

He hadn't told Pascal that the Palm Springs trip was definitely on. Edward didn't look forward to the backlash, but they'd become friends. And Pascal was part of Joe's life, though often overlooked, as Pascal put it. A side dish that you nibbled.

They first sat in the big wicker chairs out on the backyard veranda, for a quick glass of white wine, and watched for cardinals.

One sip and Edward jumped in, "Just let me explain it all first before you start analyzing..."

A couple of months max. In a condo. A friend, a retired priest in good standing, would cover the parish, live in his house. He hadn't told Joe yet. Or Cy.

He winced briefly, taken aback by the diffuse pain that sometimes wrapped his feet. Neuropathy was starting to settle in. He sighed and thought of Jesus on the cross. This was another burden for him to bear. The reckoning with a body that had lasted long on HIV meds.

But he still had dreams. And he was going to follow this one. One of the next steps had been to tell Pascal.

The words had come out easily after all. The plan didn't seem so odd for an aging gay man with HIV who wanted to relax in a welcoming climate.

Still, for once, Pascal's face was hard to read. He was looking at the lilac bushes and maples. His head was nodding up and down. That could be a good sign.

"So?" Edward needed to know Pascal's reaction, his ideas.

"You don't want Joe to forget you," Pascal finally said, his tone quiet and moderate. "You love Joe and you want him to know it. Your way of expressing this emotion is…somewhat dramatic." Pascal arched an inquisitive eyebrow. "Don't you think?"

"Dramatic in a bad way?" Edward asked, arching a wary eyebrow back.

"I don't honestly know," Pascal answered after a brief review. "I do know that inertia is an enemy to love, whether it's chaste love or lusty love. Inertia eats love and creates discontent. This I know very well."

* * *

Oscar remembered the touch of Joe's hand on his knee. It had been there only a moment because Oscar had reproached Joe, but the thought of that contact still aroused Oscar. He was having trouble putting Joe on one of the little shelves where he held all his clients and useful friends, picking them off to "dust" only on occasion.

Oscar wanted love. He would be twenty-four soon. He kept saving money, planning to study more to become certified in massage therapy. He was strong. His hands were large. People liked him to touch them. He could make the transition to legitimate massage, maybe work at Two Bunch Palms or one of the spas, maybe learn medical massage.

Then he'd find a place of his own and entertain the men of his own choice. Right now, he was at the library in Sunrise Park to recharge his phone and check his email. It had been a bad night with no client to let him stay over. He needed some food. Well In The Desert would be by soon. Maybe he'd call Richard. Richard always enjoyed his company. He was eighty and walked with a cane but still loved to suck a hard cock and, thankfully, loved to watch him shower. Oscar was sure he'd carry images of Joe in his head if he had to get hard for Richard.

And maybe Richard would feed him. Or they'd go to Manhattan in the Desert. Richard loved that restaurant, loved shuffling in with a hot young man at his side.

Yeah, he'd call Richard, get the day going before the library guard kicked him out. And it looked like a summer storm was coming. He'd need shelter for the night.

* * *

Joe was waiting nervously outside a bustling lunchtime Sherman's Deli, finding a wedge of shade as shelter. Both Cy and Luis seemed happy he was having this date. They called it a date. It wasn't a real date, though, Joe had to remind himself.

Kenny had moved on.

But Joe hadn't. Not really, although he did feel less emotion when Kenny's name came up in the exasperating inner examinations that had completely replaced his prayer rituals.

He remembered his private exchanges with his confessor, who often asked if Joe really knew his deepest feelings. Out in the desert sun, he blinked and admitted to the soundness of that probing question, that it wasn't just some nattering his confessor had gleaned from a morning talk show.

Then he saw the truck. Same Ford F-150 as back home. It said "I'm masculine and assured," or something along those lines. His pulse began to race.

He watched as Kenny took a spot on the street, carefully checking the curb and the car behind him. Had Kenny seen him? Joe was outside and squelched the urge to wave. What a kid he was! Like going to Disney.

He watched Kenny exiting the truck's cab.

His heart lodged in his throat.

And then Kenny was on the street. Tan shorts, tight tank top, ball cap, and reflective sunglasses. Clean-shaven. A nice bulge that nothing could hide. A stride to show it off. Joe's Kenny.

Then reality struck.

This meeting was now becoming a major mistake. Joe's desire had flipped to high burn. Damn it! Damn his luck! He needed to cool off. Cool his emotions. This was not a date!

Now Kenny was there. Neither of them held out a hand or moved to kiss. But something wild in Joe said, "Give me a hug, mister." And, out on Tahquitz, they embraced as if they were brothers, chaste and separated below, Kenny leaning down and over, as it always had been.

A moment. No words. What was Kenny thinking?

They separated. Had Kenny pushed off?

Kenny took off his dark glasses.

"Are you hungry?" Joe asked, finally able to look long into Kenny's sky-blue eyes. He saw a twinkle.

"You bet! I just drove nonstop from San Diego. I need a total refill. Let's go," Kenny said, putting an arm around Joe's shoulders.

Wow. That felt good. Being owned by this man. Being led by him. Joe would have to think long and hard about just this moment. He made a mental note.

Kenny greeted the hostess as if he were a star. She smiled back with a showy happiness and led them to a table by the windows.

"Coffee?" she asked, looking only at Kenny.

"Two," he answered, with a knowing glance back at Joe. Kenny was used to getting the attention of women, especially those he smiled at with that full, broad prairie gleam.

Joe was feeling it too. Kenny had a primal pull, something more than sensuality. This guy was rooted in his manhood.

Joe scanned the restaurant, noticing how people seemed to take in the pair of them, which amped up his nervousness.

Now, what next? This was Kenny's apology time.

Joe unwrapped his utensils and put the napkin in his lap. A server, another older *tío*, came by with coffee.

Neither of the men spoke. Both seemed content to examine the other. Joe was running through a whole set of opening lines, but nothing quite said what he wanted to say. Of course, that was the main problem. What did he want to say?

"Thanks for coming" finally came out.

Kenny's face immediately darkened as if a squall had blown in from nowhere. Was he going to cry?

The waitress, an older white woman with a harried look, showed up just then, taking a brief step back when she saw Kenny's face. Joe gave his two eggs order, and Kenny managed to ask for pancakes without breaking up.

As the waitress left, Kenny looked back down at his coffee, sheltering the mug with both his large hands. Joe didn't say anything. Instead, he looked out at the quiet street. It was another hot day. He could see Kenny's face in the window, a hazy reflection. He could see Kenny's eyes look at him, take him in. They were such sparkling eyes, but today a pool of sadness caught the light. This was totally the wrong place for their first encounter.

The food arrived quickly as if by magic. Both dug in, and Joe could feel the concern drain from Kenny as he loaded up on carbs and sugar.

Joe decided they should hold off on the apology and whatever might follow until they got away from the distracting whirl of movement and chatter in Sherman's. They needed a place where they could spill out their emotions in a safe zone, away from strangers' ears and eyes. Joe thought of driving to a park or just stopping on the side of the road down South Palm Canyon. It would be hot, but mostly they'd be alone.

"You finished?" Joe finally asked. Kenny looked up and nodded slowly. "Let's pay at the counter. Go someplace else to talk."

"I'll get the tip," Kenny said, still serious.

"You do want to talk, no?" Joe asked as they exited into the heat.

"Yeah."

"Do you want to go to a park, just to walk around?"

Kenny smiled. "It's seriously hot here, Joe. Don't you have a place we could go to?"

Joe looked down at his watch. Luis wasn't home. His apartment wasn't much. But he didn't know what it meant to invite an ex-boyfriend over. He didn't want to take a false step again.

"Sure," Joe said, silencing his concerns. "It's not much. You can follow me."

During the drive, Joe tried to devise an approach, how to deal with Kenny in breakdown mode. This was not the encounter he had hoped for.

On his way to Palm Springs, he had hoped this meeting would

change them both as if the sight and smell of each other would work some magic. But now he was here driving down Sunrise, uprooted from everything he had been. And this beautiful young man, the enigma of him and the allure of him, was in pain.

Joe pulled into the visitor parking area so Kenny would know where to park. Part of him had wondered if Kenny would zoom north, heading to the I-10 and then winding home on the other side of the San Jacinto range. But he was there, feet away. He hadn't offered the apology yet.

They parked and started toward the apartment's entrance. Joe hoped no one would be at the pool. They could talk in the shade cast by the second floor. It was too tempting to go upstairs, to be near a bed and a closed door.

Kenny was looking around, smiling. "Nice digs, Joe." At least he could talk again.

"I've got a roommate. The guesthouse supplies us the apartment, part of our pay." Joe squinted back at Kenny, taken in again by the beauty he had thrown away. "Do you think you could manage sitting outside in the shade? I'll go up and get us some waters."

"Yeah, that would be wise," Kenny said, chuckling. "I don't think Jasper would want me near your bedroom. He's kinda jealous that way."

They went down the front walkway, through the gate and into the courtyard, which was blissfully empty on this scorching day. Joe left Kenny to sit in the moderate shade of the south lounge area and hurried upstairs for two waters.

When Joe returned downstairs, he saw that no one else had yet appeared, though he did see a shutter move across the way. There was no mystery here. Two old friends meeting up. That's all.

Was he making up stories now? Sheesh.

Kenny had taken off his t-shirt and shoes and seemed to be settling into one of the cheap white lawn chairs. Nearby, the flock of plastic flamingoes perched next to the south wall of the u-shaped apartment building. It was a place of cover in the otherwise sun-drenched pool area.

"I like your apartment complex," he said, his chest muscles rippling when he reached for the water.

"Thanks!" Joe said, trying to concentrate on Kenny's lustrous eyes.

It was Kenny's time to talk. He had come all this way to make the apology. Joe would wait.

A raven flew overhead and sat on a palm frond of a giant fan palm in the corner of the pool grounds. Kenny pointed up at it and said, "A visitor."

"Yeah, they're here, all over. Sometimes in crowds, usually just a couple. They can be fun to watch."

Then more silence.

Kenny finally set his water down and leaned forward, looking over at Joe.

"It's fucked up what's happened to us. The HIV, I mean," he said, looking away and shaking his head. Then he straightened up. He looked directly at Joe.

"It's my fault. I got the bug and didn't know. Thought I was immune. I really didn't play around much, but I got it anyway." He took a deep breath, holding back tears. "Saying I'm sorry doesn't seem like enough. Too little. But it's all I've got. I'm really sorry," Kenny said and started bawling.

Joe reached over to touch Kenny's knee. He was afraid to do more. He had fucked up too. He had separated from Kenny. Went cold turkey. Didn't return his calls. He had damaged this man.

* * *

Kenny didn't want to wait long to call Jasper when he got back. He parked the truck and hiked quickly up to his apartment. He sat down and fingered the phone. But, first, he opened up his Blackberry browser and went to Manhunt. It was only a game for him now. He and Jasper didn't play with others together. That was the extent of their commitment. Plus, they had to be honest with each other. No hiding any encounters. Jasper had laid down that rule, and Kenny was happy to have it. It was almost a full-bore commitment. The rule had kept him from playing around, which showed Jasper his sincerity.

As Kenny reflected on this relationship reality, he noted that the guy he called "the other mister" was online. He was built like Jasper.

Hispanic. Seemed to work regular hours, so probably stable. He and Kenny would text each other for fun. Send pics. Kenny had told the guy nothing would happen, and he stuck to that, hard as it was.

Speaking of hard, he was. He pulled down his shorts and took a dick pic and sent it to his online pal. The guy's name was Manny. They'd spoken once out at the Eagle.

Ping, back came an erection. Just the kind Kenny liked. It was all he needed to finish whacking off. Then he'd call Jasper in a more laid-back mood. There'd be no thoughts of Joe in his mind. No memory of his kindness at the pool. No memory, except for the sense of relief. It was over.

"Hey, babe, I'm back," Kenny said to Jasper, who had quickly answered the phone.

"I thought you'd be back about now. Can you come over for a chat?" Jasper asked. "We can go out for an early beer, maybe go to the zoo first. It's so nice out."

Kenny exhaled. This was what he loved. He loved being with this man who just wanted to hold hands and watch the polar bears. Perfect life.

* * *

Joe paced the small apartment with an energy swollen by confusion and loss. Luis would be home soon, but Joe needed to talk to someone else about this meeting with Kenny. About the collapse of his plan to reignite their relationship. Wasn't that what just happened? He hadn't felt this craving for help in months. He needed someone just to listen. The right someone.

Then he made the call.

* * *

Oscar got the call while he was on the balcony having early cocktails with his host. It was Joe, so he answered right away, excusing himself to go inside.

"Joe, what's up?"

"I saw my ex a couple of hours ago...and I need to talk about it."

Joe stopped, then asked, "Are you available?" He waited.

"I can see you, but not right now. We're having cocktails, then going to Cathedral City for dinner. I can text you later when I'm home. We could walk down by Tahquitz Creek Channel. We can meet at the Tool Shed. It's not far."

It was a plan. Joe sounded desperate, which wasn't the priest-man's normal tone. There was fear in his voice, fear or a cousin emotion. And Oscar knew fear and all its family—knew them well. His host wouldn't mind if he went out for a stroll later at night. Richard would be in bed soon anyway.

Oscar was early, so he saw Joe drive up in his old Honda. Joe parked on Sunny Dunes, a couple of feet away, and seemed to hurry out of the car. Oscar pushed off the wall of the Tool Shed and started walking over.

"Hey," Oscar said, unable to hide the happiness in his voice. Its presence surprised him and made him wonder what was going on.

"Hey," Joe replied, walking up and standing in front of Oscar, then shoving both hands in his pockets.

Were this guy's emotions seriously congested? Oscar narrowed his eyes and refrained from laying out a challenge or sharp quip. Something was up with Joe.

"Come on," Oscar said, "give me a hug for a greeting."

Joe took his hands out of his pockets, somewhat slowly, as if he was wondering how to hug, then stepped closer and embraced Oscar.

And not just a hug. It was an embrace to remember, full of need and desire. And full of silence too, Oscar noted, which he thought was the best way of expressing what felt too hard to say.

Two minutes passed. A couple of patrons walked by and stared. Neither said anything.

Finally, Oscar uncoupled and moved back, afraid his imminent erection would start to move things in the wrong direction. "Let's go for a walk. It's a beautiful evening. And after last night's storm, I'm sure we'll hear the frogs sing in the creek."

Joe cocked his head as if he didn't know such a place existed.

"It's just two blocks. Here, give me your hand," Oscar said, getting up the nerve to grab for what he wanted. The hand of a good man.

Joe's desire to tell someone about Kenny's visit, a pressing need filled with Kenny's form and tears and Joe's dismay, had nearly vanished in the presence of Oscar. A startling development.

And now he was holding this beautiful young man's hand. The young man was towing him toward what must be a special place in this curated city.

Joe didn't know what he wanted to say now. And Oscar wasn't asking. He, too, must have been content to walk in the darkness, hand in hand.

What would Joe say anyway? That his ex feels bad for infecting him? That Joe still lusts after Kenny? That Joe knows he wounded Kenny too?

They stopped for a moment when they reached North Riverside Drive. Oscar smiled and looked over to see Joe's reaction. The sound was amazing, so animated—the bracing nighttime croaking of frogs. For a second, the creek's warm, marshy smell broke into the desert's indifference. Joe inhaled the healing scent. Then he smiled back at Oscar and moved to face him.

"My ex came here to apologize to me, you know."

Oscar's head tilted slightly.

"He had infected me. I'm HIV positive because of him," Joe said, immediately hit by the gloom of that pronouncement. "And he feels so bad about it. He's miserable, upset. I don't have the words."

"I'm sorry this visit was so distressing," Oscar said, his head almost close enough to kiss Joe.

"And it's clear we're not getting back together," Joe said. He paused a second, savoring the nearness of Oscar's warm skin. "Kenny didn't show any interest in our old relationship. So maybe it was a mistake to uproot my life and come all the way here." Joe sighed. "I acted on a fantasy. A fantasy I concocted that even I don't believe in anymore."

The two stood still with their eyes locked on each other. Then Oscar leaned in and kissed Joe, full on the lips. It was the first kiss he'd had in—Joe couldn't remember.

Oscar kept their lips together long enough for something to spike in Joe. It was a warmth and a tenderness, which he expressed by kissing back and placing his hands around Oscar's waist and pulling their bodies together.

* * *

At work there was little chatter between Luis and Joe. Joe was in a meditative mood, and Luis was not one to pry, unlike their employer.

Cy finally called Joe into the office. Joe knew Cy couldn't wait to hear what had happened with Kenny. Cy was a man with a need for gossip. An addiction, maybe.

Cy stayed behind his desk, his post of authority. Joe stood in front of the sleek modernist pine writing surface, covered now in neat stacks. Everything was in order in Cy's office. Not at all like the disarray in Joe's own life.

But, right now, Joe was thinking of happier moments. Of seeing Oscar. Of the embrace. Oscar was kind and gentle. Held him close for a long time—hours, it seemed—but it had only been minutes. Then they walked back to the Tool Shed. Oscar said they'd talk again.

"Call me," Oscar had said.

He had meant it, despite the HIV and the shadow of Joe's relationship with Kenny. Joe felt safe with Oscar. He could talk about anything with the young man. He had made his first good connection in Palm Springs.

"How was your meeting with Kenny?" Cy finally asked, sounding perturbed that he had to begin with the most obvious question.

Joe half expected Cy to know about his kiss with Oscar, so vast was Cy's network of informants. Cy was a kingpin in a large group called Prime Timers, a supporter of the Golden Rainbow Senior Center, a past president of the Desert Business Association, a sustainer of the Desert AIDS Project, and a sometime stroller with the Front Runners. Someone Cy knew could've been looking out the window at the Tool Shed and then dialed Cy.

Joe smiled, thinking again of their public embrace last night, which would probably give Cy the wrong message.

Joe hadn't spent time thinking about Kenny. The meeting with Oscar had hurried that tragedy out of his mind. Honestly, though, part of Kenny's image lingered on the outer edges.

"I'm going to say it was uneventful," Joe finally said, shifting on his feet. He knew he was giving off the vibe of someone hiding a truth. But why did he have to tell Cy about the apology? And the crying? And the sense of desolation he'd felt afterward?

"It was good to see him, but I don't expect we'll spend a lot of time together. No plans were made."

There. That should satisfy the gossip maw. Enough spin to show the direction of that relationship without any details.

Cy sat quietly as if he were contemplating a different truth. "I'm sorry that it wasn't more," Cy finally said, thoughtfully nodding his head.

"Thanks," Joe said, suddenly moved. It was almost as if Cy had hoped Kenny would've ridden up on a white horse and taken Joe away into the sunset.

"You can get back to work now," Cy said, putting an end to the awkward meeting.

Chapter 9

Edward had made the decision a month ago. Today, he stood in his bedroom sorting items to take to Palm Springs. The online forecast told him to pack for summer temps even though fall was around the corner. He would put in a warm jacket anyway. He'd bought two new swimsuits in hopes of enjoying that warm sun. The owner of the condo he was renting assured him the complex had multiple pools and several large spas. He'd finally be able to become the pool addict he knew lived inside him. Water soothed and nourished, didn't it? Even in the desert. Or especially in the desert.

As for other kinds of dryness, Edward had finally started talking to Joe regularly. Twice-a-week early evening calls for Edward after Joe had finished working and was home relaxing by his pool with Luis and other denizens of what sounded like a gay retirement club.

Joe seemed happy that Edward was coming for six weeks. In fact, Joe sounded happy, unlike the Joe Edward had first met in the HIV-positive clergy support group. That group still went on but had become more challenging after a member had killed himself and, then, Joe left. A new member, a Lutheran pastor, had shown up three weeks ago in tears and angst. The meetings with him there had been tough. This guy was a wreck without hope and lacking in basic HIV facts. Edward had reached out, but so far, the new man was too afraid to make contact outside of the group's secret meeting space.

Edward had kept Joe up-to-date with these happenings, but Joe was becoming less interested, turning the conversation elsewhere. His life seemed to be filling up with new friends, especially this Oscar he talked about. The two of them seemed to have coffee frequently, meet for happy hour drinks, and take hikes. Nothing too expensive. Exactly the script of Edward's dream when he conjured up his time in Palm Springs. Was this Oscar a new love interest now that Kenny had become another blip?

Edward didn't think so. Oscar was younger. And an escort. Not the sort of person Joe would hook up with. Joe liked guys who worked during the day and came home at night to dinner and who liked wrestling in the bedroom. At least that described Kenny. But Joe sounded happy with Oscar. Maybe he was treating this relationship as a ministry.

Whatever. Edward would be there soon, and he'd see for himself.

* * *

Cy was looking forward to Edward's arrival. And not just because he hadn't seen him in years or that they had always hooked up when Edward had been in town. Cy planned to use Edward as a pawn in his game. And the goal of this game was to separate Joe from Oscar. This friendship between the two irked Cy. It had burrowed into his skin like a spider bite, leaving a toxin that became infected and painful.

Cy felt a need to protect Oscar. And even though Cy had offered Joe sanctuary from his personal storm, Cy didn't feel any attachment growing. Joe was perfectly fine as an employee, but he seemed distant and wary of Cy. It had to do with Oscar and with Cy's warning about transmitting HIV. But it was a warning that had to be given. Cy cared deeply about Oscar as if he were his son. Except that he also used Oscar for sexual release.

Oh well, no one was perfect. Cy did his best. And his best was pretty damn good. People in the desert loved him!

* * *

Joe met Oscar at Wang's that Friday. Joe was in a good mood. The crowd there was bustling. His eyes were taking it all in, like the proverbial kid in the candy store. But he had Oscar with him. Protection. He wasn't alone. And Oscar introduced him to his friends, many of whom were clients.

Joe knew that Oscar worked the room. Oscar would cast his eyes about to see an old man off by himself. Then he'd scoot over until he was next to the guy. They'd start chatting. After about ten minutes, Oscar would pull out his business card and hand it over. The old guy would nod his head, and Oscar would depart.

"You don't feel awkward doing this?" Joe asked after Oscar returned from approaching a man who was only visiting Palm Springs for the week.

"I'm a salesman. It's my business, you know. You clean and scrub, I massage and entertain." Then Oscar tickled Joe in the ribs, causing Joe to bend over laughing. Others stared at them, but Joe didn't care. He was always happy to be with Oscar, even if the young man had something of a reputation.

"So, your friend Edward is coming tomorrow. Are you excited?" Oscar asked.

Joe hesitated, thinking of Edward. Edward was something else. He took another sip of his Bud Light.

"I am excited. He's excited. We haven't seen each other for a while. So there's plenty to catch up on. And we have a similar background. We're comfortable."

"Yes, Father," Oscar said with a grin.

Thankfully, the young man rarely used that honorific. Joe didn't want to drape himself in that cloth again. Not right now.

Edward had made arrangements to celebrate at St. Paul in the Desert Episcopal on Sundays. They welcomed him, as they had in the past, and he was hoping to work with HIV-positive parishioners while he was in the desert, a new pastoral field for him. There was something special about Edward, aside from his stature and long beautiful face. He was graceful. Gracious. A wonderful eyeful. He was especially stunning when his azure eyes glinted in the sun. It was as if a piece of the sky had settled atop them.

"What are you thinking?" Oscar asked, breaking into Joe's reverie.

Joe shook his head and breathed deeply. There was a new emotion in his reflections about Edward. "I was thinking of Edward. You'll like him. Great guy. Very kind. Approachable. Easy on the eyes, for an older *anglo.*" Joe thought that final bit was a joke, but it sounded snippy coming from his mouth, the sort of thing a drunk twink might utter on a rough night.

Oscar gave him a look, a "what did you just say?" look.

"I'm sorry. I was trying to be funny."

"I like older *anglos.* If I didn't, I couldn't do my work."

Joe put his hand on Oscar's neck and squeezed lightly. "Then you should like Edward."

"Maybe he'll be a client," Oscar said, smiling lasciviously at Joe.

Joe stepped back in surprise. Was that a likelihood?

"I guess it's a possibility," Joe finally answered, his voice a little quiet for the din of a Wang's happy hour.

* * *

Kenny couldn't shake the sadness. It followed him everywhere these days. A good-morning cup of coffee and a McMuffin didn't dispel it. A slap on the back from his coworkers did nothing. A warm Jasper smile worked for a while, but then Kenny was overcome by gloom. And night, that was a bad time, dark in the worst way.

This gloom had reappeared soon after his meeting with Joe. Why? He couldn't figure it out.

Jasper suggested he should see someone. Like a counselor. Maybe contact the LGBT center.

But Kenny didn't want to walk into their local center and say "Hey, I'm HIV positive. I infected my old boyfriend. How can you help me?" He didn't want the shame of it. Or that someone he knew might see him there and ask "Hey, dude, what are you doing here?"

Kenny didn't know what to do.

* * *

Edward's plane landed an hour before the fall sun began to set beyond San Jacinto Peak. Perfect timing for entering the warm and dry embrace of Palm Springs—just as the desert city's temperatures began to moderate but warm enough to congratulate flyers who'd worn shorts on the plane from the Midwest. That's what Edward thought at the baggage carousel as he looked down at his hairy legs. He'd rent a car, then head off to the rental condo at Sunset II, which was not far from the Smoke Tree Village shopping center. He'd be in walking distance to Joe's apartment at Desert Arms, even though the blocks were immense. Never mind. Everything about this trip just seemed to fall together. Even the rector of St. Paul in the Desert asking him to do an in-service for those living with HIV. That would give him a purpose here. And Edward needed a purpose in his life. He always had.

The biggest snag was Cy's insistence on trying to set up dinner dates and shows. Edward didn't need an entertainment director. He was here in Palm Springs to be with Joe. To say something to Joe about his feelings. Or maybe simply to let a hug last a little longer, see where that went.

Edward wasn't confident, but there was hope.

He'd settle in; then tonight, he and Joe would head out to dinner. A perfect way to start his time in Palm Springs. A little beer or wine and Joe's lovely face. He hoped Joe was looking forward to it. He had sounded that way on the phone.

But Joe could be hard to pin down. He had a lot going on inside, however hard it was for him to name much of it. He was such a talented administrator, but not skilled at putting his feelings into words. Edward understood that now. His approach would be more cautious this time. He wouldn't let Joe feel caged. That's what happened on their disastrous trip down the river back home.

So tonight would be cocktails and dinner. They'd talk about Pascal. Maybe even call him. It would be very low-key.

Edward drove in his rented red Ford Fiesta to pick up Joe. He'd had a nap and was refreshed, ready to meet Luis and see where Joe lived. Edward took Sunrise to East Palm Canyon. It took less than a minute;

traffic was light. The sun had gone down, and the streetscape was dimming, but he was able to make out the apartment number.

"It's very lovely," Edward said to himself as he stood in the courtyard and took in the calmness of the pool and the stateliness of the California palms that were lit from below. "I could see spending hours out here," he said quietly, his mind drawn into the symmetry and the pleasant dryness.

Luis met him at the door. Another knock-out Hispanic man, but older than Joe.

"Joe has been so happy that you were coming," Luis said, which made Edward's heart fill, even if it were only a courteous man's statement.

Joe was standing nearby, looking at him peculiarly as if Edward were an unexpected but intriguing visitor. Then Joe seemed to realize how offbeat his silence had become and reached over to touch Edward's elbow. "I have been happy."

Edward's eyebrows shot up. "It's great to be here finally," Edward said, storing Joe's reception in his memory as he tried to sound casual, "to spend a few weeks and do some work. I've only been to Palm Springs as a tourist. I hope to learn more about it on this visit."

"It's a town," Luis said, smiling. "And it has a lot of gay people in it, which makes it unique. For us," Luis said, delicately touching his chest, "it is magical."

"Well, I'm ready to get fairy-dusted," Edward said, laughing and leaning over to embrace Luis and, then, Joe.

"We've lots to catch up on, my friend," Joe said, finally taking the verbal lead. "We should get going."

"Let's go to Bongo Johnny's," Joe said as they settled into Edward's car. "It's on Arenas. It's a grill, but the food is supposed to be good. Guys at the guesthouse like it. Okay?"

"Sounds good. Anywhere we can sit and talk," Edward said.

Parking was easy that night. Not much was going on at the surrounding bars.

They were greeted with a warm welcome and chose to sit outside. Two other tables had older gay guys who nodded at them as they walked past. Edward started to relax. This was perfect, like a neighborhood diner.

It didn't take long for their Coronas to arrive.

Edward looked over at Joe and dipped his bottle for a toast. "To our friendship."

"To our friendship," Joe responded quickly.

Then Edward's phone rang. He'd promised Pascal to call that evening, so he picked it up to check the caller id. "Sorry," Edward said, making a "What now?" face at Joe. It was Cy. Edward froze. Awful timing. He chose not to answer and let the phone ring, annoying himself and everyone else nearby. When it was done, he shut it off.

"What's wrong?" Joe asked.

"It was Cy. I didn't want to talk to him. Not right now." Edward had already spoken to Cy after he arrived and settled in. That was enough for one day.

"I saw you grind your teeth," Joe said, grinning at Edward. "You're usually so sanguine."

"I'll settle down." Edward took a couple of deep breaths and kept his eyes on Joe. That was a good thing about their friendship. They were comfortable with each other to a degree.

"I'm not having the best relationship with him," Joe said, blocking Edward's attempt to kick Cy out of his mind. "I think I've gotten myself into a situation."

Joe's voice was steady and unperturbed, but his words set Edward on edge. He had facilitated Cy's offer of help for Joe. He was a player in this game.

Their meals arrived at that moment, and they both started to eat. Edward was hungry.

After a few bites, Edward launched back into the Cy topic, much to his distaste. "So, can you tell me more about the situation?"

Joe looked at him, somewhat shyly, as if he were a child about to admit a wrong. "It has to do with a guy."

Edward stopped eating his burger and set it down. He sat back quietly and listened as Joe explained how he'd met Oscar and how they'd become friends and how Cy had warned him off because of the

HIV, even though they were not intimate. Joe was living like a monk as regards sex.

After Joe finished, Edward leaned forward and resumed eating, trying to concentrate on his food. Two questions, however, tore through his mind: Had he already lost Joe? And had Oscar replaced Kenny?

"Quite a story," Edward commented. "I can see why Cy was so happy that I was coming to visit. Maybe he sees it as an intervention," Edward said, laughing quietly, having figured out Cy's ploy. "It's not an intervention, though, not on my part. I only want what's best for you, Joe." Edward straightened up in his chair, tensed his body, and looked Joe directly in the eyes. "What's best for the man I care about. The man that Pascal cares about, that so many people care about. We only want what's best for you."

Edward leaned back into his chair, still tense, his breathing shallow. Those had been hard words to say. They were words of support, maybe pastoral, but reciting them seemed to hollow out his soul.

Joe sat back, too, pushing away his empty plate. "Thank you, Edward. I'm glad to hear you say these things. It means a lot to me. I think your concern and...now your actual presence is one of the driving forces for my recent happiness," Joe said, opening up his palms. "Luis has remarked on it—that I'm going to see Edward, a friend from back home." Joe stopped a bit and beamed. "And I want you to meet Oscar. You'll like him. He's more than just a struggling young hustler. He's a vibrant young man. He's become a friend."

* * *

Joe's spirit glowed. Edward had driven him home, and they had sat outside by the pool for half an hour. They'd called Pascal—whom they knew would be waiting up for a call—from their loungers, speaking softly and regaling him with the beauty of the evening. Then Edward had begun yawning, and Joe sent him home. It was all very peaceful.

Joe sat content on his bed. He fondled his phone a second, thinking briefly of texting Oscar, who had wanted to know how things went. But it was nighttime, and Oscar worked nights. So Joe contented himself with switching his thoughts between Edward and Oscar, happily considering how well the two would get along.

They were scheduled to go out on Friday to Wang's, where Edward and Oscar would meet. Till then, Joe would keep plugging along at Casa Vista Oro and his daily routine. Edward had to check in with the Episcopal parish tomorrow and see some other friends tomorrow night.

Joe got ready for bed. As he lay down, listening to the whir of the ceiling fan, he suddenly realized, in a welcoming fog of near sleep, that he hadn't thought of Kenny in days.

* * *

Edward parked in St. Paul's lot, got out, and stretched his back. He looked over at the church and the office with the connecting cloister walk, breathing in and feeling a sense of satisfaction. He enjoyed this combination of Southwestern architecture and Mediterranean structures, set amid the greenery of Old Las Palmas, where the large estates of the wealthy stood seductively behind walls of leaves.

He had been to the parish on earlier trips, noting that its congregation skewed old but had plenty of gay folk. Of course, the epidemic would be hovering around here as a retirement spot for those from Los Angeles and the Bay area. Some of that diaspora would be in the pews. For an unknown reason, maybe Cy's influence, the rector had asked him to work with the congregation to establish a support network rooted in faith and spirituality. That request delighted Edward.

But as he continued to look around at the church grounds, Edward felt a sharp tinge of fear, a moment of anxiety, and leaned back against the car door. He rarely hid his HIV at home, but he also never made it a focus. This ministry would be different. It would force him to be more visible. More of a public symbol. And, of course, people would talk. The Episcopal Church was a little family, with members constantly circulating. This fear, which he didn't remember packing with him, stopped him outside in the nearly empty parking lot.

He leaned against the car a while, imagining next steps, imagining the faces of people he'd never told about his health status, his infection.

Yet he remembered that, long ago, he had chosen to be of service.

Then, shuffling off the weight of self-reflection with a practiced mental shrug, he straightened up and trod toward the office door.

Walking down the short cloister, he quickly repeated a new mantra: This is Palm Springs. It's time to breathe free.

When he opened the door, the receptionist, another gay man with a welcoming smile, greeted him warmly. Edward stood a moment and, relieved, thought, *This may not be so bad.*

"Hello, I'm Reverend Edward Brockton. I'm here to see Rector Smyth. Is she in? I'm here about the HIV support group."

Reverend Smyth was a short slender woman with dark shiny hair in a bob cut. She wore light-blue clerics and dark pants, all very Episcopal and cordial to Edward.

"I'm so excited you're willing to work with us, Edward," she said, as she turned to walk him slowly down a short corridor to her office. "Mark Lee, the gentleman who will carry on when you leave us, will be here in about half an hour. He's retired. A former Catholic seminarian. He worked in social services, so he's well qualified from that angle. But we think your presence will make a statement. Garner some attention."

In the office, Edward sat down, the rector across from him. She offered coffee, but he had already had plenty. His gut was struggling with her comment "Garner some attention." He wanted to help people open up and maybe offer them the solace he'd found in his prayer life and in his faith in a higher power whose touch he had felt. And Edward firmly believed in the value of opening up to friends and family. Still, as he'd fretted out in the parking lot, he didn't want to become a reality TV star.

But she was so excited. "We've announced it in our bulletin and website. We created a flyer, too, that one of our members took to San Diego, where he spends the week working on the Marine base. He's a friend of Cy's, Mike Regenato. You probably know him. Well, we've had a young man from there contact us! Imagine! He might call you to discuss the sessions. We gave him your number. I hope that's okay."

Aha! That would explain the call he had had earlier from San Diego. A young man who was all nerves.

Edward felt the blood drain from his face. The rector stared at him with a look of concern. Inside his head a noisy flight of questions circled and called out.

Could that man from San Diego be Kenny? Would it be a conflict of interest for Edward to lead a group with Joe's ex pouring out his soul?

And the mention of Cy. It seemed out of place somehow. Worryingly.

* * *

Jasper examined the flyer Kenny had brought home. He seemed perplexed. He and Kenny were seated on the sofa, embracing, doing nothing special, hanging out.

"What are you thinking?" Kenny asked.

There was a pause. The big man was weighing his words.

"I appreciate that you're making an effort to deal with this HIV diagnosis. It's been hard for you. Awful," he said, rubbing Kenny's inner thigh. "Still, this doesn't seem to be the type of group that would appeal to you. You're not religious, not that I know. I've never heard you talk about prayer. Or God."

Kenny shifted so he could get a better look at Jasper. "I wasn't really religious as a kid. Standard Lutheran upbringing. Bible study. Singing...lots of singing!" He laughed at the memory of the choirs he'd joined. He had a nice voice and could read music. He hadn't hated Sundays. Going to church was just part of being with the family. Until he moved out.

But...now. He had tried to grab onto something inside himself, just like he'd read in the self-help pamphlets he'd managed to pick up. But every handhold of wisdom he grabbed onto seemed to crumble after a while. Jasper was the best, but Kenny still felt like Jasper was an inspecting officer at attention on the parade ground. That was okay, of course, because they were getting to know one another.

"The flyer said you didn't need to belong to a church or be a true believer. It said the meetings were for explorers, people looking for spiritual resources," Kenny said, hearing the defensiveness in his voice.

He was afraid to say that he'd always felt comfort with a guy like Joe, a priest, and that he wanted to find that kind of comfort somewhere. How do you say that to a guy you're falling for? He couldn't.

"What's going to be different about this group?" Jasper asked. "Isn't it just a prayer group?"

Kenny looked out the window. He knew there was something in that group for him. The priest.

Chapter 10

On Friday, Joe drove Edward to Wang's. They'd been hanging by Joe's pool in the evenings. Spending time with Edward had been almost as stimulating as being with Oscar.

But those two hadn't met yet, the pair who now comprised the two sides of Joe's social life. So tonight was the night. And why was Joe nervous? They were both his friends, no? Except Oscar made his living with bodywork, and Edward made his with soul work. Joe joked that his friends had different ways of relieving tensions and clearing blockages, but that simple wordplay did little to relieve Joe's concern about this one point: Joe really wanted them to get along.

Oscar was going to be a few minutes late, so Joe and Edward got a drink and found a good corner by the red Buddha where they could talk.

"I'll finally get to meet Oscar!" Edward said. "I just wonder if I'll be able to hear him!"

The music was as loud as ever at Wang's, but the blaring sound hadn't reduced the crowd: the locals who turned off their hearing aids and the visitors who came to see, to be seen, and to jostle their way through the crush. Joe felt the excitement of it, but now his mind was on this one meeting. He wouldn't be hunting for Mr. Right, a concept he had recently begun to explore with lists on a notepad. Kenny's visit had made one thing clear: he didn't have much of a chance finding a partner. He was used goods, scrap on the slag heap of sexual misfortune.

"We don't have to stay long. One drink, then we can head out to a quieter bar," Joe answered, speaking above the clamor. "Oscar likes to make an appearance here. Maybe chat with some guys he knows. I'll let him explain it."

That last bit sounded ominous. Joe didn't want to say Oscar used Wang's as a marketing tool, a place to hand out his card and glad-hand, to show himself off as someone attractive but nonthreatening, someone you could invite into your home. He'd let Edward figure it out.

Joe nodded at a couple of guys from the guesthouse who had been friendly with him. They were standing by themselves and didn't seem to want to chat, which struck Joe as odd. At Wang's, people mingled. Maybe it was his status. Lowly worker. But he caught them eyeing Edward as if they'd like to snatch him up. Joe suppressed a smile. That would never be Edward!

Then he looked at Edward and saw he was smiling back at the guys. So, Joe thought, Edward was playing the game of desire. And he played it well, dressing his slim frame in well-fitting clothes, smiling gently, keeping a bearing that spoke of his worth.

And, then, there was Oscar coming in from the parking lot in shorts and tank top, showing off his lanky, muscled frame. He had waved to an old guy seated across the room. Joe nudged Edward. "There he is. He's going to say hello to that guy over there. Then he'll come join us."

Edward's eyes lit up as if he hadn't expected Oscar to look the way he did. Joe was afraid to ask.

Edward leaned down and spoke into his ear. "He's gorgeous."

Joe smiled at Edward, thinking, *Yes, he is. And intriguing too.*

After an hour at Wang's, Edward insisted the trio go down to Arenas. They ended up dining at Bongo Johnny's—Edward's treat—after the other two had demurred, citing cost.

"I'm hungry and I have two good-looking men to dine with. Please! I'll pay," Edward said as they stood outside on the sidewalk. He was now in the middle, and all three of them had their hands around each other's waist. Everything seemed perfect in the welcoming mildness of a Palm Springs night in the center of gay commerce.

Edward didn't want to let go.

He wasn't sure how the touching had started, but for Edward, it was a benevolent spring rain.

Joe and Oscar looked at each other as if they could decide on his invitation with just a glance. Edward chuckled. These two really knew each other.

"Okay," Oscar said, moving forward. "I never refuse food that is offered with a generous spirit." Then he kissed Edward on the cheek.

Once they were seated, the conversation centered on Oscar. Edward knew the shoals to sail away from, such as Cy, and Oscar's living arrangements and the way he made his living, and Joe's HIV and his ex.

Edward regaled them with Pascal's latest interest, knitting. "He says he's preparing himself for a useful old age!"

They all laughed, but Joe looked thoughtful. Edward knew that Pascal felt Joe had abandoned him, driving off to Palm Springs in search of love. "Love in the dust!" Pascal would say as if he were referring to an ancient civilization that would never revive.

"I would like to meet Pascal," Oscar said, dipping a French fry in a dollop of ketchup. "He seems to be a good friend to both of you. I admire his taste in men," he said, licking his lips.

Chapter 11

Edward was in his condo, busily getting ready for his first meeting with the HIV positive support group at St. Paul in the Desert Episcopal. His afternoon moments of concentration and speculation were only broken when he stopped to gaze outside at the park-like grounds and at the palms that framed views of the slopes of Mount San Jacinto.

He had made copies of the agenda and quotes from relevant sources: rabbis, priests, ministers, and a few HIV-positive people he knew with testimonies of hope. The first night was sometimes the easiest. The group would be diverse with one thing in common, a disease—a disease with a messy history of tears and destruction.

Then Edward sensed impending danger.

So he paced.

Edward knew why he was nervous. That one issue loomed, large as the mountain he could see out his patio gate, devouring the horizon.

He had not yet figured out how to deal with the potential Kenny issue, deal with it in a way that didn't drive a wedge between him and Joe.

Membership in this group was confidential, so he couldn't discuss Kenny's participation with anyone. Not even Pascal, who had already discerned he was holding back something, something that was still developing.

"Have you met someone else?" Pascal had asked in the morning's phone call. "Is it Oscar?"

In a way it was Oscar, Edward thought. That first night he'd met him, he'd recognized the desire inside. It glowed like the desire for Joe. And this, this awkward similarity, made him try to tamp it down. Find faults. Observe flaws. It brought out something harsh in him.

"Pascal, you bloodhound!" Edward had said, letting Pascal know he was on the scent, but not giving away too much. Then he thought maybe Pascal could help him sort it out.

"He's very much like Joe. Inordinately attractive. More personable than Joe, I'd say, even though Joe can turn on the charm. Oscar has it in spades. Maybe developed through his trade."

Edward had waited for Pascal's response. How would Pascal, liberal as he was, view someone in the sex trade?

Surely Pascal knew how lucky he was. Despite owning only a few hangers of clothes and having a pittance in the bank, he did have a warm spot to rest. The Catholic Worker house was a real home. So he had more security, in that way, than Oscar.

"I'm not going to judge him," Pascal had finally said, his tone slightly cool. "But I will say his presence is complicating your life."

Ha! Oscar's AND Kenny's presence complicated his life.

"He does complicate my life. He makes it harder to..."

"To get Joe to see that he loves you," Pascal had said, finishing Edward's thought.

* * *

Five people showed up for the first HIV positive support group meeting at St. Paul in the Desert; they huddled on chairs in a meeting hall at the back of the property.

A young man came in last, after four older guys had settled into chairs, said brief hellos, and started to look at their watches. When the door opened seconds before the start time, all heads turned.

He was striking, just as Edward had imagined. And he was nervous. Edward hurried out of his chair and over to the door to welcome him before the new man had a chance to turn and leave.

"I'm Edward. I think we spoke on the phone," Edward said, putting out his hand.

"I'm Kenny," the young man said, standing stiffly near the doorway.

Edward's blood flow ceased for a moment, making his heart beat harder when it started again. This was Kenny. Kenny was here, just as Edward had feared.

Then he looked closely into Kenny's eyes and saw the flashes of fear.

An impulse to help flamed up inside Edward, burning away other thoughts.

"I hope you'll join us," Edward said, then leaned in closer and whispered, "We can talk alone after the meeting, if you want."

The meeting ended with a brief silence, allowing the attendees either to pray or to plan their next moves. Afterward, Edward hesitated briefly, then placed a hand on Kenny's arm.

"I won't keep you long, Kenny. I know you've got a long drive," Edward said, catching the worry and fatigue in Kenny's eyes. He pulsed his hand and released Kenny's arm. He wished he could provide Kenny a bed for the evening, but knew that would be completely inappropriate.

"I know this was a hard evening for you," Edward continued, offering the consolation of concern and an opening for dialogue.

Kenny brushed his hand over his short-cut hair. Edward observed how the shape and size of his arm muscles punctuated how beautiful this young man was and how vulnerable.

"Tonight," he said, gesturing to the room, "was hard. Listening to those old dudes. It just dragged me down more. You know?"

Edward nodded his head slowly, acknowledging what had turned into a somber and bleak sharing session. "I felt the same." Best to be honest. "But I hope we can get beyond telling these pain stories and start to explore ways to deal with the mess we're all in." Edward stopped a moment, opening and closing his hands. "I know I've been able to do that. One learns." Edward had started the meeting by stating that he, too, was HIV positive. "Some have even made this diagnosis the cornerstone of a better life. But staying upright, engaged in life—that can be a challenge, I won't deny it."

Kenny looked at Edward as if he'd said something meaningful. He gave Edward a brisk worker's nod at a job well-done. "It can be hard to keep going...," Kenny said, blinking moist eyes, "hard to keep all the parts of my life functioning, keep hope alive."

"You have hope...," Edward said, intoning a question.

"I'm not despairing," Kenny said, smiling. "At least not yet."

"I won't press you to come back if you don't want to," Edward said, offering Kenny a way out even though the minister inside Edward wanted Kenny to come again. "I wish you didn't have to drive so far. And I wish the group hadn't started out so rough. We didn't get to discuss anything spiritual, as in a spiritual practice, which is what I had hoped to explore. You know, ways to deal. Not just reciting prayers, but everyday practical acts."

Kenny laughed. "I could use some help dealing." Then Kenny looked down at the floor. "I could use someone to listen. It's not just HIV that bothers me. I've got an ex. And a boyfriend. I know who I want, but..." Kenny's eyes watered and he brushed his hand over them.

Edward waited.

Kenny lifted his head and looked at Edward.

"Maybe we could talk again after group. Next time," Edward offered, acutely uncertain about opening a pastoral relationship with Kenny. But even ten minutes alone might help Kenny.

Kenny finally answered. "I can't come next week, but maybe the following week. Then I'd like to talk more."

Edward stopped at Hunters for a beer, unsettled by the group session. The bar's evening crowd had thinned out, which he had anticipated, and he was able to sit at a table near the street-side windows and reflect. The music and lights didn't bother him. He welcomed them, the little distractions that kept his mood from spiraling down after a tough first meeting. He kept looking outside, watching the few guys walk by and the trickle of traffic. On a weekend or holiday, the street could be packed. But tonight was a regular night in Palm Springs, warm and starlit, a feeling of tranquility in the air.

Edward sipped his beer. He wondered if Kenny would even come back at all. The young man was still in that early frenzy of diagnosis:

unsure, afraid, looking everywhere he could for answers that didn't contain the words "chronic" and "incurable." Adding to that cocktail were his relationships, which were churning his emotions.

Edward took another sip. And then he saw them.

Oscar and Joe, walking down Arenas Road. Not hand in hand, but with bodies that touched on occasion. Walking foreplay. They were laughing, and Joe was smiling. Oscar seemed to be regaling him with some funny story.

Edward, not moving, held his breath.

Cy's call woke Edward from a deep sleep. Even the sun hadn't been able to stir him. Thoughts about the first session and the sighting of Joe and Oscar had kept swirling through his brain. He had finally managed to fall asleep sometime after three.

Edward was groggy. His imagination had expected Joe to be calling.

"How did the session go?" Cy asked, full of gleeful interest as if he had known that Joe's ex was attending. Edward certainly hadn't told him of his suspicion.

"Uh, good morning. Sorry, I'm not too coherent this morning. Everything went okay last night, for a first session."

Edward knew Cy had championed the idea of Edward taking on this duty and had lobbied the vestry and rector to support it. So, it made sense for him to be interested. But so soon?

"Was it a big turnout?" Cy asked, still probing.

"Five men," Edward answered warily.

"And a man from San Diego?"

Edward was stunned and scrambled from his bed. Had he mentioned that fact? Or was it the front desk staff dropping a little gossip.

"Uh, it was a diverse crowd. I can't get into specifics, you understand. Confidentiality was assured."

This was so awkward. Cy had been such a good friend. More than a friend, a bedmate at one time.

"I see," Cy said, sounding as if he had garnered a "yes" from Edward's answer. "I'm glad you've found something to do here in Palm Springs. I have always thought you'd make a wonderful rector here!

If the day should come..."

Edward cringed. Was that it? Did Cy want to staff the church completely with his drones?

"I appreciate your confidence in me, Cy, but I'm just here for a short time, maybe a couple of months. A break from my routine."

"Yes, I understand," Cy said, almost with a drawl. "I hope to see you tonight at the Prime Timers' mixer."

"Same here," Edward said, eager to end the inquisition.

The call had displaced his thoughts about Joe, but they rushed back in quickly enough. Edward was becoming worried about Cy's influence. What could he do to Joe? Joe needed the job; he needed the security of paycheck and apartment. Edward had seen Joe laugh last night. This was a good direction. But Cy's scheming—it was an ache in Edward's stomach.

Chapter 12

Kenny snuggled next to Jasper on the Marine's long sofa. A police drama played on the TV. Two beers, the remnants of a pizza, and their entwined legs covered the coffee table.

Kenny was still recovering from his trip to Palm Springs. His distress must have shown because when Jasper had first seen him, he'd said: "Whoa, soldier, you look a goner."

Kenny had chuckled but knew what Jasper meant. He could feel his skin drooping.

On the sofa, nestled next to his man, Kenny noted his deepening appreciation for the big fella. Jasper didn't hector Kenny with questions. He didn't want to talk about *it* all the time. He made plans to be with Kenny. And kept them. That was Jasper, a man of his word. When he invited you over for pizza and a beer, you could count on the beer being cold and the pizza hot and cheesy.

So why was Kenny so sad? He found himself cuddling with a hot Marine. A man who clearly liked him, who invited him into his home, despite his status.

Something had happened at that meeting. He knew it. Something had bruised him. Kenny didn't understand what that could be. Hadn't he gone to Palm Springs to learn how to handle this disease better? Maybe learn to pray about it, if that were even possible. Wasn't that the solution he needed? Instead, the other men's stories of pain had sent his emotions spiraling down, a plane out of control. The engines had flamed out.

"You feeling any better?" Jasper asked during a commercial, looking at the TV instead of at Kenny, leaving Kenny to ponder his question unobserved.

"I'm feeling great next to you. Otherwise, I'm shit." Kenny looked at Jasper, who was now staring at him. "I'm sorry for being such a buzz-kill. I can't seem to get myself beyond it, whatever 'it' is."

Jasper rubbed Kenny's arm, surfing over the blond hairs, back and forth the way he liked, as though he were examining some new exotic furnishing. Kenny liked the feel of his touch and Jasper's attentive concentration. It made Kenny feel wanted and appreciated. Of value.

"I wish I knew what to say," Jasper finally spoke. He muted the TV and shifted an inch more toward Kenny. "You know I want you at my side. I could take a thousand nights like tonight. And then another thousand until we got old. That's what I feel."

Tears gathered in Kenny's eyes. "Thank you," he said, not sure that thanking Jasper was the correct response, but he felt he'd received a gift.

Then he felt Jasper tighten slightly. "Are you feeling the same?"

The question of the hour. Of course he had to ask it. Jasper liked certainties.

"I'm gonna be honest," Kenny said, moving back a bit. "I've been hurt, and I don't want those feelings again. Look, I moved halfway across the country because of them. But right now, on this sofa, I don't want anything or anyone other than you. I'm falling for you."

Then Kenny leaned in and put his hand up to Jasper's face, softly stroking the stubble.

It didn't take much, that most intimate touch, and they were back in Jasper's bedroom. This time the sex was slow. Oh so slow. They both felt it. Some new energy had wrapped around them, warm and with an easy pulse.

Later they lay exhausted in the silence, listening to the few car doors out in the parking lot and the occasional bark.

Finally Jasper pulled his hand up Kenny's treasure trail where a hint of red darkened it, something that so fascinated Jasper, just as it had Joe. He hunched up on one elbow, his hand still moving up and down. He stopped where the cum had begun to dry.

"I think you should go back the week after next, when we don't have plans," Jasper said, his voice now crisp with its Marine certainty. "But let's make it simpler for you. Let's take a couple of days in Palm Springs. You won't have to drive back at night. And maybe you can book some alone time with this reverend. What do you think?"

<h1 style="text-align:center">Chapter 13</h1>

Joe had begun driving by himself to Casa Vista Oro, even though Luis had offered to keep taking him. He liked the control it gave him. On the trip there, he could check out the scenery and stop every so often to admire the landscape. He was absorbing Palm Springs with a new freshness. Over lunch, he sometimes just went to wander along Tahquitz Creek Channel. With his after-work plans, which had included Oscar and now Edward, he was experiencing even more parts of the city. Luis didn't mind either. Maybe he was relieved that he couldn't report on every detail of Joe's day. He was a good man, Luis, and Joe was sorry that there was tension between them. But he understood Luis's position. His roommate was, in many ways, an indentured servant, working and living at the whim of his master.

Joe didn't want that life. He'd unshackled himself from a clerical prison and wasn't about to strap on another set of cuffs.

And things were going well. Very well. At least emotionally. He rarely thought of Kenny now. Instead, his mind dwelt on Oscar. And now on Edward. They were going out together again this Friday. Wang's, then dinner. It would be great. He was going to see Oscar this evening, meeting him at the house where Oscar was now living. It belonged to a retired physician who was on a European jaunt and had paid Oscar to live in, walk the dogs, and watch over the place.

It was the sort of gig that was common in Palm Springs. But, for a young man, the barrier was trust. That's how Oscar explained it.

Old men see him and wonder what he wants. And knowing Oscar as he did, Joe knew he primarily wanted a roof over his head and something to eat. A good young man with a keen insight into the motivations of others.

If he'd met Oscar back home, Joe could've found a place for him. He would've hired him at one of his outreach foundations, managing food for the homeless or helping to keep peace in the women's shelter.

* * *

Cy took the call. It was from a butch Marine, and his heart started to flutter. He wanted to reserve three nights.

"Is it a special occasion? Should I prep the room with chocolate and flowers?" Cy asked.

The Marine laughed. "Thanks for the offer, but we aren't celebrating anything special. It's just a time to get away and relax. Every couple needs that."

"Of course, of course. And your partner's name?"

Cy wrote down all the information: credit card, Lt. Wylands' phone number, and his partner Kenny's full name, although Cy wasn't sure he wrote the last name correctly. He'd have to spend some time with them when they arrived to clear up the details. And he had an inkling there would be details.

Their stay encompassed the evening support group that Edward ran. They were coming from San Diego. One of them was named Kenny. The Kenny who now worked at a Marine base?

Cy's lips started to curl. Did this Kenny know who worked at Casa Vista Oro?

Delicious!

This plan was working. Cy had given Mike Regenato a special offer to share with gay officers at the Marine base, and Jasper had bought it. Cheap midweek digs. It was a special aimed at only one target market.

* * *

Oscar greeted Joe with a "Welcome home, honey" and a kiss on the lips, a kiss that lingered. It was their second lingering kiss; Joe was keeping track.

Stuck on that count and unsure how to read this greeting, Joe's inner guy engine rumbled with a definite desire to keep kissing, to move his hands up to Oscar's face and hold him there.

Instead, Joe stepped back, silent. The surprise in his eyes probably reflected his emotions better than anything he could say.

Oscar put his hands on Joe's shoulders and said, "I'm sorry. I was just trying to be funny. And welcoming. You're...you're confused."

Then he took Joe's hands and led him inside. "You've got to see this place! The modernist pixies have been at work here! White leather Barcelona chairs. Atomic light fixtures. Blond wood. Mainly whites and grays with funky, angular, colored art—I guess you'd call it art. I tell you, living in Palm Springs is a gay boy's education!"

Oscar's patter didn't loosen Joe up, so Oscar sat down on the sofa, gestured at Joe, and patted the spot next to him. "I think we need to talk. We have time for cocktails, but let's talk first. There's a tension that I want to address," Oscar said, eyeing Joe now seated next to him. "Are you okay with that? I'm pretty sure you feel the tension, too, unless something has gone totally wrong in my wiring." He laughed, a happy and unalloyed laugh.

However, Joe sat and stared with a watchman's gaze. Was it the priest in him, or was it merely the man in him that started to tick off the cautionary points: Oscar's age—early twenties; the few weeks they'd known each other; Joe's health status. Neither of them had much of a career, and Joe didn't have a clue how to proceed.

So Joe didn't say anything. He fiddled with his hands and mindlessly bit his nails. And then he reached his left hand over toward Oscar and placed it around the young man's shoulders and nestled his head on that firm shoulder.

"I'm enjoying the silence," Joe finally said, sounding stupid but honest. He wasn't ready for too many words, too much definition.

Oscar reached over and patted his right leg. "It's okay. I am also."

Five minutes passed as the mourning doves sang their plaintive evensong, and Joe could feel his heart beat in rhythm with Oscar's.

Then Oscar spoke softly, "But you're a serious guy. And serious guys have to talk about things, or they get screwed up inside. I may be young, but this I know. Because I'm a serious guy too." Oscar turned to look directly into Joe's face. "What's going on inside that pretty head of yours? And don't worry, I'm not telling anyone. It's confessional talk."

Joe looked into Oscar's glistening brown eyes, which had no mischief in them, only kindness.

What to say?

"It's my fault," Joe said, beginning with guilt. "I cultivated you. Your friendship. I wanted it." What Joe wanted to say was that he feared he was toxic. He was hearing Cy's voice. "Maybe I'm using you. I'm sure part of me is."

Oscar shook his head as if he couldn't believe what he was hearing. He got up to look outside as the evening outdoor lighting blinked on. He spoke to the outside. "As I recall—and perhaps your demon has erased this from your memory—I sought you out first. What you feel is not wrong, wanting my friendship. To know me better, to know me closely." He paused. "I am a willing participant." Then Oscar turned to face Joe in the dimming light of the room. He bent to turn on a table lamp. "Joe, you don't have the resources to offer me a haven or security. Not the financial resources. But you do offer me something I value. You respect me. You enjoy me for myself and not just my body, which you have not known. And I think you're starting to love me, as I am starting to love you."

Joe froze, his mouth agape. He contemplated the love word and repeated it inside his mind. He had once used it with Kenny and then fouled that relationship. But the urge was there, inside him. The urge to use the word again.

Finally he spoke, "Everything in its time, I guess. It's just I...I need a little more time."

Chapter 14

Cy called at 10 a.m. just as Edward was heading out to the pool. Cy said he had a gift for him.

"Cy, just being here feels like a gift. I'm off to the pool to relax and gaze at this amazing mountainscape." Edward hoped that jabber would put Cy off.

"It's something that is special. And dear to me. It's a massage!" Cy sounded like a happy child, which made Edward even more nervous. "It'll be by someone I'm bringing along in the trade. After all, we have to cultivate these lovelies here in the desert, or we'd be a truly barren landscape! If you accept, he'll show up around 10 p.m., just before you head to bed—if I remember your habits properly."

Edward considered it a moment. He had that lower backache that hit him in the mornings. And tension in the shoulders. His chiropractor kept telling him to relax more and recommended some stretching exercises he could do in a chair. Chair yoga, they called it. But Edward didn't think he was quite that old. Or infirm.

"Okay, okay. I'd be happy to provide my body for training purposes," Edward said, laughing brightly as he approached the pool gate. "I'm at the pool. Text me the details. Thanks, Cy!"

Only after he'd spread out his towel and lathered up did Edward have the thought. Could Cy be setting him up with Oscar? Would he do that?

And what would Edward say to his masseur when he showed up?

Well, he could laugh it off if the masseur was Oscar, and the two of them could have a drink and a chat.

Anyway, it would all work out, whether the masseur was Oscar or not. Oscar could handle anything. And Cy would be paying him. After all, Oscar needed money. It kept him afloat.

* * *

Joe stopped at Edward's after work. Edward had invited him for a late afternoon swim in the pool followed by an ache-relieving dip in the spa, and then dinner. They could boil up some pasta and munch a salad. Much like Oscar, Edward had quickly become a keystone to Joe's happiness in the desert valley. Interesting and beautiful as Palm Springs was, he still needed someone close to help him mark the experiences in his soul, someone who would share the little things, a cactus blossom at the pool or the first moments of relaxation while entering the spa.

Edward was the perfect guy to help Joe experience the world around him. They were so comfortable together, had a past together, could even have a future together—somehow, in some shape.

As he got out of his car, Joe thought about their evenings out with Oscar: the laughing, the casual touching, the pleasure of listening to Edward and Oscar's banter. Their relationship was a blessing that was blossoming. They were three friends, happy as a group and happy as pairs.

Joe rounded the sidewalk to Edward's rental, and there was Edward waiting! He was standing at the patio gate as Joe walked up. He was in shorts and flip-flops, a towel over his shoulder. He could've been a model for a Palm Springs retirement calendar. Tall, lean, and smiling. And sexy.

"Did you bring trunks?" Edward asked. "If not, I have an old pair that should fit if you pull the string tight."

"I scooted home and put on a pair. Lead me to your pool," Joe said with a broad grin.

He went through the gate, then quickly pulled Edward into an embrace accompanied by a peck on the cheeks. Back home, he had been wary of any touch; such was the state of the Catholic priesthood after all the scandals. He had learned to keep his hands immobile at his sides.

Edward seemed surprised, off-kilter by this embrace and kiss, Joe thought. Was it just his newness to this city where open affection was normal? Or that this quick move on Joe's part was so out of character? Joe swore to himself to keep it up, to keep up being open in his affection.

"I've got us some Gatorade on ice and two loungers shaded by a table umbrella," Edward said and smiled.

Joe laughed and glanced at his arms and legs. "My skin has darkened since I've been here. I rather like the look." It was a comment he could never have made back home, so self-aware—or body aware.

After an hour at the pool and spa, they went inside, where Edward had the central air set at seventy-eight.

They stood in the entryway in their wet trunks, cooling and drying. Edward looked over at Joe, just a tick longer than custom, his eyes unmoving. Joe started to feel himself harden—an odd development since that had never happened with Edward—and he moved his towel in front.

"Come, have a shower," Edward said, quickly shaking his head and motioning down the hall. "I'll just change into some ratty loungewear, if you don't mind, then get started on dinner."

Joe smiled, relieved that the moment was passing. "I'd love a shower. I'll be quick! And food sounds great."

"Refreshed?" Edward asked as Joe came into the kitchen.

"I am," Joe said as he walked over to where Edward was slicing an heirloom tomato. Without thinking, he put his hand on Edward's shoulder.

Edward stopped for just a second as if he were assessing the touch. Joe smiled, enjoying the moment with his old companion. He liked Edward and he wanted to show it. Oscar would approve.

Then Edward got his pace back.

After dinner, they took their beers and sat out on the shady patio; darkness was coming to the Valley. Edward turned on an overhead fan attached to a small trellis. It stirred the calliandra that grew up the side of the patio and added coolness and a welcome rustling of leaves to the evening. A few condo dwellers were walking their dogs and waved as they passed.

"It's peaceful here," Joe said, releasing his breath as if he were exhaling years of frustration. He reached over and put a hand on Edward's knee. "Thanks for letting me come over."

The silence deepened.

Edward was looking at him when Joe said, "You're very special to me. I'm so happy to have you here right now."

The sun was down, but Edward was basking in the presence of this new Joe, this man who was at ease, this man who had learned the art of touch.

So he didn't want to bring up the massage. Or Cy. But some dogged orthodoxy inside him wouldn't stop its muttering. The subject needed airing. After so many years, he was still a guardian of truthfulness.

He coughed to get Joe's attention.

"Cy called today," Edward finally said, making his admission in a hushed, confessional voice.

Joe jerked his head and sat up.

"It's not about you!" Edward quickly added. He didn't want Joe to think he was a conduit for Cy's micromanaging.

"Good," Joe said, sounding relieved but threatened. "I'm not comfortable with that man, to be honest. I appreciate what he's done for me, but I get the feeling that he's playing some game. And then that thing about the tattoo. I told you, didn't I?"

Edward nodded his head. The tattoo incident was one more jagged rock in a pile he'd been gathering. "That was certainly a misdirected anxiety," Edward said.

"But I did tell Oscar about my HIV...afterward," Joe said, this time reflective and quiet. "Maybe it was then that our relationship deepened. After we'd both shared intimate facts."

"A good thing coming out of misery," Edward said, looking over at Joe, wishing he didn't sound so clerical.

"So, you were saying about Cy calling?" Joe said, getting back to the thread.

"He's planned a gift for me. A massage."

Edward could see Joe's body stiffen immediately, his arms tensing and his jaw tightening. Joe swept his hand through his dark hair, the way he always did when upset.

"You know what he's doing, don't you?" Joe said, anger in his voice now. "He's sending Oscar to you. He wants you to use Oscar the way he does. Maybe it's a form of absolution he seeks, absolution via collusion, in which you'd use Oscar the way Cy uses him. Or maybe it's a pawn move in a game we don't understand."

"I thought the same, except for the absolution part."

Joe sighed. "What are you going to do?"

"I'll let the masseur, Oscar or not, give me a massage. That would be a treat. But we'd limit it to a regular massage. It is a legitimate trade."

Joe had gone, and Edward started to wander in the condo as thoughts darted through his mind: the greeting Joe had offered—an embrace with a kiss—and the unavoidable massage. His certainty that the masseur was Oscar and the anticipation of being nearly naked with him was making him sweat. Maybe he should shower.

Then Oscar was at the main gate, arriving right on time, as Edward had expected. The lad was efficient, sharp, and handsome. Edward buzzed Oscar in.

Edward stood in the dark patio, awkward and uncertain, nervously reciting: a massage is a massage.

And, suddenly, Oscar was alongside him. He was carrying a table, which was a nice surprise.

"A friend is helping me learn the trade," Oscar said, immediately interpreting Edward's reaction.

Just like the young man to intuit his thoughts.

"And another friend lent me his car," Oscar added, chuckling as he carefully maneuvered the table through the door. "I'm blessed with good friends!"

"Yes, you are blessed to have good friends," Edward answered as he closed the door and stepped into the living room. He vowed to avoid any discussion of Cy. He didn't want that schemer to be part of this evening. "And I hope you count me as one of your friends."

"I do," Oscar said with a smile before he turned around to scan the setting for the best spot to place the table.

"Do you want to have the massage here? We could close the blinds. There's plenty of room for me to set up," Oscar said, gesturing to the living room.

"This would be fine. Let's move the coffee table and put your massage table there."

Together they silently flipped the wooden coffee table onto the sofa. Oscar opened his massage table and set it up.

"Do you like scented candles, or is it too warm for that?" Oscar asked.

"I'm Episcopalian. Of course I love scented candles!" Edward said, then wondered if that reference had any meaning for Oscar, a *Latino* from a vastly different culture.

But Oscar laughed and brought out his candles and some oils from the bag he'd been carrying. "Smells and bells. I get it. One of my first clients was a Catholic priest who went on and on explaining points of religious trivia. I'm well schooled for you."

Edward smiled but felt a twinge in his heart. He knew so many clergy were out there prowling for touch, for approval, for what appeared to be love. He'd been one of those prowlers himself during the last years of his marriage. Not a fact that made him proud.

"You okay?" Oscar asked, sensing his mood.

"Yes, I guess. Just reflecting on choices. Some of them wrong."

They both stopped and stared at each other.

Oscar broke the silence, pointing with both hands back at himself, "This is not a wrong choice, Edward. You deserve to relax. And I deserve the practice." Then Oscar bent down and reached into his bag to pull out a wrap towel whose length had been shortened. Handing it to Edward, he said, "You go undress and put this on. I'm going to warm up the oils a tad, light the candles, put on the music. If you don't mind, wet your hair but don't dry it. Come out when you're ready."

Edward took the towel and studied it briefly, raising one eyebrow. "Sounds good," he said and walked back to his bedroom, shutting the door, almost locking it, and then wondering why he felt so prudish.

He knew he wanted this experience, even fantasizing briefly about Oscar's hands slipping past a boundary of mere friendship. But he had promised Joe the massage wouldn't go sexual, a promise that might be dampening his spirit.

Edward undressed in seconds. The towel fit him nicely, making him wonder if Oscar kept a stash of them, eyeing his client and pulling out the right size. Or maybe this wrap was only for the more squeamish clients.

He checked his form in the mirror before going back to the living room. He turned in profile. He nodded at himself. He was still in good shape for his age.

Returning, Edward was pleased with the setting. Oscar had managed to dim the living room, lighting it only with a handful of candles. Celtic fusion music played in the air. Plaintive, but not too sad. Edward felt some of his tenseness drift away. Oscar knew how to set the scene.

Oscar instructed him to lay on his back for the first part of the massage. "I'm going to start with your head and shoulders, then your feet and legs. I won't speak, but tell me if you want me to do more of something or less of something. You can close your eyes or keep them open. Either way is fine with me."

Soon Oscar's face was over Edward's as Oscar gently began to massage Edward's temple. Edward closed his eyes and instructed his mind to be quiet, to find a god-like setting and sit there.

Edward noticed his breathing. It started to slow. He inhaled the scent of the candles and breathed in the scent of the oil now being rubbed into his hair and over his scalp. He paid attention to all the tiny movements of Oscar's hands. Each one now anticipated with pleasure. He could feel the muscles of his face loosen up.

After massaging his feet and thigh muscles, Oscar finally asked him to turn over, an act he dreaded, exposing himself to a touch he so wanted but couldn't ask for. Edward noticed his breath was now choppy. The mood was changing.

But not for Oscar, for he cooed "Relax" several times into his ear.

Then Edward felt the pressure from Oscar's elbow on his lats, and he let out a low rumble.

"Okay?" Oscar asked.

"Oh yeah."

Chapter 15

The night had finally arrived. With each passing day, with each report of Joe and Oscar's growing closeness, and now with Edward's increasing involvement, Cy became more and more impatient for his plan to succeed.

So anyone with a clear view into Cy's inner self would understand why he sat restlessly as he waited for Jasper and Kenny to arrive at Casa Vista Oro at 9:30 pm. Their instructions were to ring the buzzer at the guest parking gate for the small parking lot behind the property, and a housekeeper would greet them. The brochure specifically stated the guesthouse didn't have nighttime staff but would make arrangements for late arrivals. Sometimes that would be the owner Cy, the brochure explained, because he lived on the compound and enjoyed meeting arrivals.

Cy watched the security camera intently as the two young men got out of the car.

"Nice looking," he mumbled as he rose from his chair. They'd probably get their gear from the back and then walk up to the door. He'd seen it a thousand times. He'd be ready. The way he was always ready. Cy knew he had a gift. A gift of foretelling. He could see the future, and he was pleased with what he saw.

He was halfway to the gate when he heard the bell. It was quiet in the compound, and the small sound rang out from the office.

"Welcome," Cy said as he opened the gate's door, standing back to let the two brawny men come in. Yes, these were specimens. Fine. Fit. They probably would never vacation at his guesthouse, but the special offer he'd arranged to send to the gay Marine officers put a guest suite within their reach. Cy only hoped they didn't talk to the other guests about the sale price. It wasn't his normal business practice to discount anything.

"I'm so glad you could join us," Cy said, staring into Jasper's dark eyes, well-set in a squared-off Marine face. "I'll show you to your suite."

"This is perfect timing for us," Jasper said with a large, warm smile.

It always is perfect timing here at Casa Vista Oro, Cy thought. Vacation. Relaxation. Luxury resort.

"I hope you'll find your stay at our guesthouse relaxing," Cy said as he moved down the walkway. He always wanted guests to enjoy themselves. That sentiment derived from his good business sense and his basic kindness toward others. However, this act of luring the two unsuspecting young men to Palm Springs twinged his conscience. He knew he was setting up drama. Drama for the man he was trying to help after an HIV diagnosis. And drama for Oscar whose life had become entwined with that of the new man. And probably drama for Edward, who seemed to have become the third wheel in Joe and Oscar's busy social life. His manipulations were piling up and starting to smell, even to him.

"It's lovely in here," Jasper replied.

The man is an officer and a gentleman, Cy mused and purred.

* * *

"This place is making me nervous," Kenny said after Cy had closed the door and left them with their keys. Kenny wasn't sure he wanted to stay.

"Why?" Jasper asked, looking stunned.

"It's posh. Very, very nice. This front room is larger and nicer than your or my living room. And that guy. The way he kept staring at us. It just left me feeling wrong."

"It is nice, babe," Jasper said, "and we can afford our stay. We'll be fine. Let's give it a try. If it still feels wrong, we'll bolt."

* * *

Joe was alone and sitting outside in the darkness at the apartment building's pool. A threesome had gathered to drink and laugh over in the southwest corner, but Joe only waved and said "Hi" and kept to himself. He wanted to reflect, quietly, with deliberation, if that was a skill he still possessed.

What had become of him? He had launched himself on this journey with an urgency, a magnetic force that drew him toward Kenny. Kenny meant life. New life. Renewed life. But their meeting was a disaster. A confession. That's what it was. Not the reunion Joe had dreamed of.

But that night Joe had reached out to Oscar, made his own confession, and now...now he had a new urgency in his life: a desire to get back in the game, to do something good with his life, and just maybe, to find his soul's partner.

* * *

Jasper was up first, as always. Hard and ready, but unwilling to force Kenny to wake and mate. They were on vacation. There would be other times. Maybe he'd go to the pool for a dip.

Outside, the sun was fanning over the top of the building. The birds were out. Sparrows and crows sang and cawed in their morning chorus. Jasper loved this time of day. He loved waking up to see the earth's rotation shake up existence and brush away sleep.

He dropped his terry cloth robe on a lounge chair at the deep end of the pool and made a shallow dive. Naked. What a luxury!

Jasper stayed at the deep end, pumping his legs, then gulped down a couple of drafts of air and dove. He opened his eyes in time to examine the pebbled bottom of the pool and smiled. It was a saltwater pool. Gentle on the human form. And the flooring was first-rate.

Up he came to the surface and started his laps. He'd do ten, then rest. See how he felt. Maybe another ten. Best to have a plan.

Jasper's primary plan for this trip was to make Kenny wake up.

Wake up to the life they could have. Wake up to living with his HIV, not dying with it.

Wake up, Kenny, he thought as he turned for lap three.

* * *

Kenny started his morning stretch: toes to the end of the bed and hands as far back as they would go. They hit the padded headboard, which he used to stretch his fingers.

No Jasper, of course.

The man was up early.

Up.

Kenny was up, too, and wishing Jasper was here to help him with that. He decided to leave it till later and pulled on his underpants. Then he shuffled over to the bedroom window and opened the plantation shutters so he could look out.

He saw Jasper's robe at one end of the pool and his strong, black arms pumping along the surface of the pool, his head shifting from side to side as he took in air. The man knew how to swim.

Then Kenny caught a glimpse of movement at the shallow end of the pool, near the office, where there was a gate to the guest parking. An older Latino walked in and quietly shut the gate. First, he looked into the pool. Kenny saw his eyes widen, something he'd come to know as the black-man-is-here expression. Jasper had taught him to look for it. If only they knew how righteous Jasper was, how much he walked the straight and narrow path.

Next, the *Latino* spotted the robe Jasper had taken off, and Kenny saw his shoulders relax. With a slight turn of the head, the man looked toward the office. Now Kenny could see that the office shutters were open, just as his were. There could have been a form back there looking out. The *Latino* made a head bob toward the window and moved on.

The other guy behind the shutters was probably an office manager up early. He'd probably gotten a great view of Jasper, a view that Kenny knew and loved.

Kenny stayed at the window, hoping to see Jasper as he got out of the pool, all muscles and luscious dark skin.

Then the gate opened again, and another *Latino* entered, a guy with a baseball cap. His eyes were down, and he didn't notice the man in the office or Jasper in the pool. His gait was athletic, his form built for action. Just like...then Kenny saw him clearly.

Joe looked up and over into the pool and smiled.

Chapter 16

Kenny stepped back from the shutters the second he realized the worker entering through the gate was Joe.

His heart started to beat rapidly, and the sweat accumulated under his arms. He wasn't ready for this. Joe here and Jasper swimming in the pool. They're going to meet. Today.

Kenny went back to the window. Joe had disappeared, a relief. For a second Kenny worried about his urge to hide. Hadn't he finally separated from Joe? Wasn't the apology the last act in that drama? He watched Jasper finish a lap at the deep end of the pool, slowing, grasping the top tiles.

Jasper heaved himself out of the water, slipped on the flip-flops, and headed over toward their room. Halfway there he met Joe, who was carrying a cleaning bucket and washcloths. He was heading toward the lounge chairs. Ready to clean them?

Kenny could hear the two men exchange hellos.

"Beautiful morning," Jasper said, always a man to start a conversation.

"Yes, it is," Joe said, stopping a moment. "Wonderful time for a swim. I hope you enjoyed it. You've got a good stroke."

Jasper laughed. "It's a big pool for such a small place. It was great to get the workout."

Then the pause.

Kenny knew the pause. Two beautiful men meeting.

"Well, I won't keep you," he heard Jasper say. Kenny heard the Marine in that reply. It had everything in it but the "Dismissed."

Kenny's mind slowed down as he absorbed Jasper and Joe's interaction. Something in that exchange cemented his resolve. He knew, for sure, that Jasper was his man, the man who had stood by him, the man who had chosen him definitively—with no qualms.

* * *

Joe was finishing up cleaning the lounge chairs and putting out the small wastebaskets for guest use when Luis shuffled up behind him.

Luis touched him on the shoulder. He whispered, "Meet me in the utility room. Two minutes."

Then he walked away.

Joe looked back at him, surprised, not knowing what could be happening now. Had he done or said something to offend a guest? Had he been lazy, caught gazing at the mountains when he should've been cleaning? Or was Cy on the warpath again about God knows what?

Joe gathered up his cleaning supplies and sneaked a glance at the office. The shutters were open, but he couldn't see any peering eyes. Then he glanced over at the suite where the hot black guy was staying. The bedroom shutters were closed now. He probably had a boyfriend in there. A guy sculpted like him? For sure.

He was putting the rags into the laundry bin when Luis walked in.

"I noticed something this morning, and I want to warn you," Luis said.

Joe stopped and raised an eyebrow. What was this?

"Yes?"

"You know I am told about guest arrivals and departures, no? Cy has a list."

"I do know that. That's how we plan our days."

"Cy told me yesterday about the two guys who came here last night. I thought nothing of it until this morning when I walked in and saw Cy in the office ogling the black guy and looking like he was waiting for something to happen."

"Okay…" Joe leaned forward, intrigued and now worried.

"So," Luis said after a pause, "I remembered their names. Jasper and Kenny. From San Diego."

Luis's message hit like an uppercut, unexpected and fast, striking a raw part of Joe's soul.

"How? I can't…" Joe couldn't get out any words. "They don't have the money for a place like this. I can't believe it."

Luis just nodded his head.

"Cy did it," Joe said through gritted teeth while pointing toward the office. "He arranged it."

Luis shrugged his shoulders. "It's possible. I don't know."

"I'm done!" Joe said, throwing the rags onto the floor. "I can't work here. This place is poison!"

"Wait. *Cálmate*, Joe," Luis said, his voice stern. "You have to think a moment. Don't be rash."

"I won't be used for his entertainment. He thinks I'm his puppet! Well, I'm not! He's tried to break up Oscar and me. He probably brought Edward here. And now this! I will not be manipulated!"

"Okay…okay, Joe, but think a moment. It's a job. You can go home sick today. Stay away until they leave. I'll cover for you."

Joe slumped down onto the floor, holding his head in his hands. What to do? Luis was right. He couldn't just walk away, could he? Surely he could find another job. A similar job. Luis would help.

The two of them remained in silence until, at last, Joe spoke. "You're right. I'll go home sick. Let me out through the trash gate, please, so I don't have to walk past Cy."

Luis nodded his head. "I'll cover for you. Don't answer your phone when he calls, because you know he will. Maybe go somewhere. Go to Edward's." Then Luis extended a hand and helped Joe off the floor.

* * *

Cy came out of his office and looked over at Jasper and Kenny's room. So far, so good. He was helping again. He was helping Kenny stay in Palm Springs and have an unrushed time at the support group.

And he was helping Oscar by distracting Joe. Oscar needed to get his act together, establish himself more firmly. He didn't need a wounded man hanging around him.

So he wasn't surprised when Luis told him that Joe had gone home sick. Cy couldn't come out and ask whether Joe had seen Kenny. He'd seen the closed bedroom shutters in Kenny's suite, but that usually meant sex or sleep, the two side benefits of being in Palm Springs.

But Luis's attitude—the way he offered the information as if there were more to it—told Cy what he wanted to know. Luis was sharp but readable. That's why Cy liked him as an employee. He knew how to translate Luis's eyes and tone into thoughts that weren't always spoken.

And what Luis had said without words was "Joe knows Kenny is here and is distraught."

And Cy smiled.

This was a good plan. Now he'd have to work on the next move.

* * *

Joe was gritting his teeth, sitting in his faithful Honda, clutching the steering wheel and squeezing it with all his might.

His first instinct was to contact Oscar, but he knew that would be a mistake. Oscar still needed Cy. He provided regular work. An entrée to his guests and to friends, reassuring them that Oscar was reliable, not a gold digger. And Cy provided money on the side for Oscar to take Certified Massage Therapist classes. Joe couldn't jeopardize that.

Cy wasn't all bad, although he was a conniving evil bastard and Joe didn't want to see him ever again. Ha! That would be impossible in this small town. And Cy had eyes everywhere!

Luis was right. He should contact Edward. He'd grab a coffee at the Smoke Tree McDonald's and head over.

* * *

Edward woke up early, as he always had since his arrival in Palm Springs. Being here was exciting, even if he didn't have anything planned.

Today, though, was a tough morning. He hadn't slept all night. The senior warden of St. Paul's vestry had called late last night. He had wanted to discuss an idea with Edward. Tomorrow morning, ten o'clock. At coffee.

Edward knew in his gut what it was about and so had turned over in his bed all night, wrapping himself in his sheets, longing for someone to hold, to offload his energy onto someone else.

He had sniffed the change. An offer was coming. A friend back home had told him the Canon to the Ordinary of the San Diego Diocese had been asking questions about Edward. Edward knew he had started this in motion by offering a few services, managing the support group—all with no salary.

He fit into St. Paul in the Desert. He checked many boxes. Gay. Clergy. Positive. Tall. He grinned at that box. Being tall had always helped him. Not gigantically tall, but tall. And lean. He was leaner now too. He'd become more active in Palm Springs.

But could he do this? How would he live? He wasn't able to retire. He needed income. He'd probably only get a part-time salary; it wasn't a wealthy parish. It wasn't St. Margaret's in Palm Desert, but it was comfortable.

And what about back home? He had a house, friends, all his old contacts. And his doctor.

The thought of changing doctors chilled him. His doctor knew him, knew his med history and his vitals and everything he was going through. And he made time to talk with him. Would that be the case here in Palm Springs? With so many old people and guys with HIV?

So many questions.

Then the phone rang.

Wow, early for a phone call. Who could it be?

Joe.

* * *

"I should've brought you a coffee!" Joe said as he walked into the condo's front patio. "I'm sorry for showing up so early, Edward. Your neighbor let me in the complex's gate."

"Joe, it's a pleasure to see you, even though I'm not quite ready for the day. I was just getting my head settled."

"If you can get your head settled, I'd love to learn the trick of it! Today, I have nothing but a rattling tin can up there," Joe said as he knocked his head with his free hand.

They stopped a moment in the middle of the patio, then Joe moved forward to hug Edward.

"Let me put this down so I can get a real hug," Joe said, placing his coffee on the small table. He rested his head on Edward's chest and reached his arms around Edward's waist.

Joe felt Edward's hand move slowly up and down his back, a soothing gesture, the way a father would comfort a child. He took a deep breath and settled into the embrace. He felt himself calm down. Felt the anger flow away. This was the gift of Edward. Edward the peace giver.

Edward the good man.

A person could do worse.

Then Joe pushed away. What was he thinking? He looked up at Edward, a bit of the wildness back in his eyes. "Do you have time to talk? Something's happened."

"I have time," Edward said, pausing, "especially for you." Edward placed his hand on Joe's shoulder, another peaceful gesture. "Let's stay out here if that's okay." He looked down at himself, "I'm just in tank top and gym shorts. This is me at rest!"

"It's perfect. I'm so sorry to impose on you," Joe said, feeling a lump in his throat.

Edward must have noticed. His voice got deeper and he didn't move, his hand still on Joe's shoulder.

"You can rest here as long as you need," Edward said.

"You've been such a good friend, and I've been..." Joe stopped abruptly, feeling the weariness and anger and despair ready to burst out.

"You've been reeling," Edward said, filling the silence. "From a terrible blow. A loss of status, a loss of your community, a distance from friends. And this disease that eats at us no matter what. You seem in freefall."

"I almost quit today," Joe said. "From Vista Oro." Then he laughed. "I guess I'm a quitter. First, the priesthood. Now, from housekeeping. Great résumé!"

Edward let go of him and leaned back to get a better look into Joe's eyes. "Tell me," Edward said.

"I ran into Kenny. Unexpectedly. At Casa Vista Oro. Jasper was in the pool. Beautiful man. So now I've seen him." Joe stared a moment at Edward, hoping he didn't sound piteously jealous or deranged. "I didn't see Kenny, but he was there, maybe looking out. Luis pulled me aside, said he'd seen the registration. He mentioned their names. From San Diego. What's the likelihood of there being two gay Kenny and Jasper couples in San Diego?"

Joe knew he was rambling, but he just kept on. "I have to say... I came here to California to be near Kenny." He paused and breathed. "That desire is pretty well gone now, so why my anguish? Because I don't want to see him with his new man? Because I don't want him to see what I've become?" Joe paused a second, looking down at his hands. "It's all so petty."

Joe looked up again into Edward's eyes. "But the other thing. I knew immediately that it was Cy. Luis knew too. That bastard lured them here. He wants to mess with me. And I know why!"

Edward reached to press Joe's shoulder. "Did you do anything? Say anything to Cy? Actually quit?" Edward asked.

Joe shook his head. "I didn't quit, but I want to. I don't want to see that man again. And I can't go back and see Kenny. It's best if we stay apart. We're separate now."

Edward was nodding his head, his eyes watchful and glistening.

Joe took a deep breath. "Can we sit?"

Edward nodded, gesturing to two lounge chairs.

"Maybe I was stupid coming here to Palm Springs," Joe said. "It was impulsive. I wanted to be anywhere but at Mater Dei. And this place seemed as good as any other. And you'd hooked me up with Cy." Joe froze. "Oh, I'm so sorry, I'm ruining your friendship with the man."

Edward chuckled. "Don't worry about that. Our relationship is complicated."

"Cy's been good to me," Joe said quietly. "Given me shelter, very Gospel. But he's still a prick. And his being a prick has to do with Oscar. I know it. In a way, Oscar is a son to him. A son who strokes him, but still a son. It's...it's something I'm not comfortable with. Or used to."

Edward nodded and watched Joe closely.

"Cy's relationship with Oscar makes me squirm," Joe said. "But Oscar protests when I even show the slightest concern. Oscar is in command of his life. That's what he says, and I know he's right."

"And you're not," Edward said, sounding hesitant. "Not in command, that is, of situations here. Or should I say, less in command than you'd like to be."

Joe raised his eyebrows. Edward's words had hit home. "I thought leaving the priesthood would make me more independent, but it hasn't. I'm still wrapped up in all sorts of webs that aren't of my own weaving, and I don't like that. Not at all." Joe smiled.

Relief threaded through Joe. Edward was helping.

"I'll have to go back to Casa Vista Oro. I know that."

They were both quiet.

Joe looked at the greenery in the patio and watched the water flow down the sides of the round fountainhead in its far corner.

"I do have an idea percolating," Edward said, breaking into Joe's silence. "Just an idea now. Almost a dream. I'll tell you later when I get back from a meeting at St. Paul's tomorrow morning." Joe tilted his head in curiosity. He had his own idea percolating, just a muddle of a thought. A reaction to Oscar's plight. A remembrance of who he used to be.

* * *

Kenny and Jasper ate breakfast at Casa Vista Oro. Kenny didn't want to spend too much money on this trip, and both breakfast and lunch were free—part of the price. He was all for that.

The breakfast area was nestled in a courtyard between two buildings. Three couples were already there, sipping coffee, nibbling on bagels, and reading through the *New York Times* and the *Wall Street Journal*.

All six heads looked up as Kenny and Jasper came in. There were six hellos, and Kenny could read the interest. He and Jasper were the hottest guys there, not something that happened much at the bars in San Diego. They hung with a muscled crowd, six to eight guys who liked to lift and stay in shape.

But the older guys were friendly and welcoming. Quickly, one of them asked for details. Where were they from? What did they do? Kenny could see the smiles on their faces when Jasper explained he was a Marine officer and had met Kenny on base. Fantasy become reality. Kenny knew the score. He was okay with it; dating a Marine was more exciting than dating a priest. Military was hot. Porno hot. Dating a priest was an involvement best not discussed in public.

Jasper seemed to fit in fine with the group. He was educated, affable, self-confident. Kenny just hung back from the conversation.

And then one of the men said to his partner. "Did you hear about the hot cabana boy, the one who used to be a priest?"

Kenny's ears became sonar, but he managed to wait calmly for the answer.

"No, what? He didn't return to the sacristy, did he?" asked the partner whose shoulders were beet red.

"Luis said that he got sick and was taking a few days off. So there goes our afternoon entertainment," the man said, leaning over to Jasper. "We'd watch him deftly prune the hedges and gather leaves and, then, wander over to stop him and ask questions about life in Palm Springs. He was a real dear! We've all told Cy he's sold us on the Vista Oro experience."

Kenny's breathing stayed regular. He smiled and kept his silence. He looked over at Jasper and winked. He felt content because the Joe story was becoming just another anecdote. Jasper had said to him earlier, after Kenny had told him of Joe's presence, that being here together was going to soften those bad feelings about the Joe separation, about the HIV. Before they left the suite, Jasper had held him tight and told him Joe was a man in pain, a man in a dark alley, but that Kenny was exiting that alley. Kenny and Jasper were exiting that alley together.

* * *

Oscar saw Luis at a *taquería* in Cathedral City. *La Esmeralda* was busy for lunch, as always. The service language was Spanish and the music Mexican and the food spicy and fast. Perfect for both of them.

Since Joe had begun his friendship with Oscar, Luis had become more willing to spend time with him. This pleased Oscar, as his life worked most smoothly when everyone got along.

"How goes it, Luis?" Oscar asked, expecting some meaningless chatter as he settled into a side chair.

"You haven't heard? He didn't call you?" Luis said, staring into Oscar's eyes as if the question were an accusation.

Oscar startled. What was that question about? "I've heard nothing."

"I'm not sure where things stand now, but Joe almost quit this morning," Luis said, his tone breathy, conspiratorial. "I think he's off somewhere cooling down."

Oscar carefully folded his hands in his lap. He was focusing on Joe and the word "quit." Joe needed this job and the apartment he slept in. Joe couldn't live like Oscar. Joe didn't have Oscar's inner steel. Or Joe had steel, surely, but it had been stressed to the yield point.

"What happened?" Oscar asked softly, eyes on Luis.

"Well, it appears that Joe's ex-lover, Kenny, is staying at Casa Vista Oro, which is amazing in itself as our clientele doesn't usually include, uh, tradespeople. So we both assumed that Cy had something to do with it. And Cy was lurking around, peeking through his window as Kenny's new boyfriend swam naked in the pool. I saw him step back from the shutters when I came in through the gate. A few minutes later, Joe came in and stood briefly examining the new boyfriend as he swam up and down the pool."

Oscar nodded, following everything, avoiding a smirky smile at Cy's cunning wiles, his ability to interfere, sometimes for good, in the lives of others.

"I knew I had to tell Joe so he wouldn't be shocked, maybe act outrageous around our other guests, so I told him to meet me in the utility room. You see, I knew that a 'Kenny' and a 'Lieutenant Jasper

Wylands' were staying with us. Cy had told me. He always informs me of new guests, their names, any issues—all to better prepare for them. When I saw the name 'Kenny,' I knew this was going to be a problem."

Oscar's eyes narrowed as he listened to the detail.

"Jasper was like a porn star. He was rippling through the water of the pool as if he'd been born in the ocean. Naked."

"A match to the fabled Kenny," Oscar grinned. "So...Joe? He got angry?"

"He felt manipulated. Yes, angry. I was afraid he would go off on Cy and there would be a scene, something ugly, something Joe would regret."

"And Cy would regret," Oscar added, a little concerned he might sound disloyal. Oscar had to be loyal, he silently reminded himself. If not...

"And Cy would regret," Luis agreed, leaning over closer to Oscar. "Possibly."

"You mean?"

"Cy has an itch about Joe. I don't know what it is, whether Joe seems too distant to him, that he doesn't kowtow to him, that he doesn't seem abjectly grateful. You know what it's like to owe someone?" Luis asked, an angry tone rumbling in his voice.

"I understand indebtedness," Oscar answered calmly. "I owe much to Cy. I can count on him." Oscar had to profess his faith, in case this conversation got back to Cy, but he also heard the resignation in his voice. The sound was more intense today, and its presence unsettled him.

Oscar pushed back his chair and moved to leave. His hunger had vanished. He wasn't sure what to do about Joe. Maybe he should let his friend cool off. Let Joe make the next move. Or maybe he should contact Edward.

Oscar walked out of the restaurant. He was sure Joe was with Edward. He'd wait to see if that pair roped him in. He pursed his lips as he decided to keep his distance for a day, challenging as that would be.

Chapter 17

Edward had insisted Joe spend the night in the guest room at his condo. Joe offered no resistance. His sunken-eyed face said it all: he craved a time and place of introspection, somewhere away from Cy's domain.

Edward had explained he would be out by ten o'clock the next morning for his meeting at St. Paul's rectory, but the rest of the day was unplanned. Of course, Joe would be free to do as he wished.

The next morning after returning from St. Paul's, Edward found Joe in the kitchen, a cup of coffee in his hand, his face blank. No, not blank, pensive.

Ready to share his news, Edward said, "Joe, let's sit in the living room."

They sat at opposite ends on the sofa. Joe said nothing, but Edward thought his eyes were wary or, perhaps, distracted.

Edward began, "Last night, I told you I have a dream, an ambition, I guess. It appears possible, now, after my meeting at St. Paul's." Edward paused a second, not entirely sure he had chosen the right path or was using the right words to explain it. "I am considering moving to Palm Springs."

Joe stayed silent, but his eyes narrowed.

"The vestry and diocese want me to work for them part-time. This would be the perfect place for semiretirement, wouldn't it?"

Edward waited for a response.

There it was, Edward's dream. His path to a dreamscape he wasn't yet ready to lay out completely.

Joe sat without moving but had shut his eyes momentarily when Edward said "Palm Springs."

Then Joe bent forward. "I didn't expect this," he said in a hushed tone. A moment later he sighed and lay back. "I have a dream too." He paused a second and blinked his eyes, smiling now. "First off, you should know that your dream makes my dream become a tiny bit more real, more viable."

Joe became animated as he outlined his plan.

Edward listened carefully and offered sounds of encouragement as he took in the shape and scope of Joe's dream. He began to like it more and more. And there was one big plus. Making it a reality would mean working together. And that was part of his path, no?

Joe asked for a pencil and paper and went to the pool. Edward watched as Joe—with the old-school pad of lined paper and a worn pencil—settled in the shade of an umbrella and scribbled. And, every so often, he stared at the mountain.

Edward thought to invite Oscar over later, after lunch. He knew Oscar's presence would help Joe mellow out. And to be honest, help reassure Edward he should commit to his dream.

Edward was surprised Joe hadn't brought up calling Oscar. Or maybe Joe was afraid to call Oscar. Ashamed, maybe.

Still, Edward would welcome Oscar's addition to the condo, his and Joe's hideout.

Before Edward could dial, Joe came in and sat at the small kitchen table with his pencil and paper and, now, the calculator on his phone. He was good with numbers and budgets, a necessary talent when working in organized religion.

Man does not live by bread alone, but bread makes life so much easier and so much more stable. And they would need many baker's racks of bread if the plan they were devising—together—was to work. It was still only a plan. A shape in the fog.

Edward stood at the patio door, looking fondly at Joe tapping away at the calculator.

Then Edward's phone rang.

It was Oscar!

"Are you up for an afternoon lap in the pool followed by cocktails?" Edward quickly asked.

"Well, I believe my schedule is free this afternoon, so I would love to join you. Would Joe be there too?" Amusement rang through Oscar's voice.

Edward grinned broadly, his face full of delight. So Oscar had heard. The grapevine was alive and well. The tendrils connecting.

"Yes, Joe is here. He's working away at the table. I hope we can convince him to don some trunks and join us."

Joe looked up and smiled.

As Edward set the phone down, he heard Joe call out from the kitchen table.

"We'll do it in phases!"

Edward was still wrapping his mind around the "it." This was new territory for Edward, who had never thought of himself as a pioneer.

Joe was the tiller of new fields.

And Edward wondered about Oscar. Would he join them in their plan? He was, after all, part of its inspiration.

* * *

So many ideas were crossing over each other or fighting for air in the tight gray maze of Joe's brain. His head was bursting with possible actions and consequences and resulting resource needs. But this was good. A stimulation he had missed in these past months. He now had a challenge that touched his soul.

Say it in a few words: build a refuge.

He could move people with those words. He, the man of God. The gay man of God.

It would start small. They needed to prove the concept. A refuge for homeless gay youth. Late teens to early twenties.

Edward had some savings. They would buy a small house in Cathedral City, a place where extended families were a reality. People coming and going. They didn't want to annoy their neighbors. They didn't want relationships to get tense, with car doors slamming and children hustled away.

They would start small. One or two guys. They'd ask Oscar to help. At twenty-three, he was no longer a teen and largely homeless. They'd hire Oscar to live in the house, like a house monitor, so Joe and Edward could be busy with other necessary jobs: scrambling for funds, dealing with the civic institutions.

They'd have to figure out the social services system in California. Oscar would need new training, certification. And they'd need money.

Which brought Cy's face into view, and Joe winced at the sight of him.

* * *

Edward and Joe sat in silence at the kitchen table, each reviewing budgetary and staffing needs if they were to do the refuge right in an idealized social services world. Then Oscar arrived. Edward buzzed him through the main gate. Oscar had biked over. He told them his current host had let him borrow an old ten-speed.

Edward helped Oscar through the condo's patio gate. He glanced at Joe through the condo's open door. He was still at the kitchen table. Joe looked up, his fawn eyes watery, and precious, and a little on edge.

Joe rose as the two of them came into the kitchen. He embraced Oscar and clutched him tightly.

Edward held back. His thoughts were on the next steps. Their plan, a word that sounded too assured now, would soon be revealed. But, in truth, it was more like a proposal. A proposal for Joe and Oscar to live together with him, to share a household, to share routines. To love each other, fraternally for sure. His palms were itchy now and his heart raced. Edward was nervous, just as he'd been when he'd proposed to his ex-wife. But now there were three of them in this proposal. Three adults at the gaming table. Each would be planning his own strategy. Or at least Edward hoped there would be three. That was the headline: the three of them together.

"You've eaten?" Edward asked when Oscar and Joe unwrapped their embrace.

"I have, but I'm hungry for news. You guys are the talk of the town!"

Edward winced. He hoped Oscar was exaggerating. They needed to be careful not to upset settled allegiances. They would need help from many others to get started.

Edward put an arm around Oscar, saying, "We'll sit in the front room and discuss what we've been planning. We're toying with ideas."

He led them both into the living room, but he would let Joe drive the discussion. For this plan to work, Joe needed to engage fully, to fight through all the funk that covered his soul.

Chapter 18

Cy couldn't reach any of them. Not Oscar, not Edward, and certainly not Joe. None of them answered. And Luis was uninformed, out of the loop. One actual bit of information Cy had was that he'd heard from the vestry's senior warden that Edward would accept their offer of part-time employment as an assisting priest and counselor. That salary would barely pay a car loan, let alone rent. But Edward took the offer. Either he was trusting in God, or he had other funds.

So Cy's immediate plan to bring Kenny into Joe's presence had backfired. Cy had to admit it.

He noticed Kenny and Jasper were outside swimming, sunning, and entertaining the older guys with their antics. That was a silver lining. Cy made a note: Invite friendly, hot guys to stay. It creates a vibe that will attract repeat customers.

Then his thoughts returned to the situation at hand, which called for a plan simply titled "undermine Joe."

* * *

The threesome had been at it for several hours. This was now work. But the willingness to pitch in, to share, to explore—it was exhilarating. For Joe, it felt better than his decision to leave Mater Dei and move to Palm Springs. Why? Because now he had two wonderful faces, two beautiful souls joining him. He was no longer working off the fumes of hope.

What most astounded Joe was that Oscar, the youngest and least experienced of them, was guiding. The young man had talent. He knew the realities of life in the desert. He could organize thoughts, rank lists, and question assumptions. And he knew the value of a dollar, especially in this Valley. His experiences moving around in households had taught him, or so he professed.

Joe was happy. He couldn't deny it. Yesterday had started out shitty, with another Cy trick. But this, this collaboration, was amazing.

However, when he mentioned renting in the apartment building where he and Luis lived, Oscar had started to laugh. "Cy owns it, *cariño*. He and his partner Matt own lots of real estate. That's where the money comes from, not the Casa Vista Oro. The Casa's his hobby!"

Joe's face had reddened, part anger, part humiliation.

He was a babe in the woods here in Palm Springs or, more aptly, a babe in a field of cactus and scrub brush.

There was so much Joe didn't know.

"So we not only have to be able to afford a place, we have to find a place Cy doesn't own. I don't want to be beholden to him. Not anymore," Joe said.

The other two looked at him, both mum.

Then Oscar spoke. "I make do with what I can acquire," he said, speaking softly, as if to a child. "I understand your feelings. Especially after yesterday. But I'm not willing to risk everything I've built here just to avoid Cy." He stopped a moment, reflecting. "It can't be done. He's everywhere!"

"He won't actively work against us," Edward said, stepping quickly into the conversation. Joe noticed how sure he sounded. "He lives in this community. He won't want his reputation to be tarnished. If he does something to break us, it will be subtle."

Joe nodded his head and smiled. "Break." A powerful word. It meant that a real union was being formed among them.

Joe began to relax after swimming a string of laps at the big pool in Edward's condo complex. Oscar had headed off to a client for a couple of hours, and Edward was inside the condo. Joe stopped to rest a few moments in a shaded corner of the pool. As he cooled down in the fresh water, he could feel his energy about the project start to come back. The only sharp thought was a feeling of disgrace that he had run from seeing Kenny. If anything was knee-jerk, that was it, a total neural response. But was it neural? What grown man acts that way?

A sad one, maybe, he thought. But why was he so deeply sad?

About to wade deeper into those questions, he saw Edward approach the pool. Edward wore a new red speedo with the Canadian maple leaf design, something one of his infatuated snowbird neighbors had purchased for him.

And it fit well. Very well.

The man was still in great shape. His walk was secure, and his smile, which now blazed at Joe, rippled out with pleasure.

Joe waved at him. "Come on in, Edward! The water's great!"

Placing his towel and a bottle of water on the lounger next to Joe's, Edward called to Joe, "Are we going to race?"

"No way! You're so much longer. With those arms and legs, you'd beat me!"

Edward laughed and entered the pool at the shallow end, then dove and swam to Joe's corner. Edward came up in the water just in front of Joe and embraced him as he rose, then pulled him down into the water, like boys cavorting.

Joe got loose and started to swim away, but Edward dove under and caught him halfway across the pool, reaching up and tangling his hands in Joe's floppy surfer's swimsuit. He was pulling it off.

Joe stopped and stood up at the four-foot point in the pool. His swimsuit was now half off, and he desperately tried to pull it up. But Edward was standing there, too, right in front of him. Closer, now, and he breezed a hand down Joe's side.

"Thanks for the romp," Edward said. "It's always good to be a little naughty."

"I knew you would be faster than me," Joe said, then dipped to fully grasp his swimsuit and pull it up over his excited cock.

How could he hide this? Thank God there were only a couple of old gay guys at the pool, guys who were happy with younger men clowning about.

But with Edward! What had happened?

There must have been some confusion in his eyes as he stood up facing Edward because his friend's eyes had changed. The glee was gone. There was an intensity in his look.

And then Joe moved his hands. Slowly and deliberately through the now still water. He could feel the eyes of the old guys watching. He saw the quandary, a blue wonderment, in Edward's eyes as he slowly placed his hands between the fabric of Edward's speedo and the man's smooth skin. He brought the speedo down below the crotch and felt the expected toughness as Edward stiffened.

Then Joe brought both hands up, one breezing briefly along Edward's stiffness as his hands finally landed on his friend's shoulders.

"We're even now," Joe said and winked at Edward.

Edward's eyes were huge now. It seemed every cell in his body was trying to calculate the meaning of the last few seconds.

Finally, Edward gulped and echoed, "We're even now."

The look of contentment on Edward's face satisfied Joe, so he dove again, swimming back to the deep end.

Chapter 19

Edward threw together a quick stir-fry for their evening meal, chopping produce from the weekend's farmers market he'd visited near Camelot Theater and adding some chicken from Ralphs. All three would stay the night at his condo. There was so much more to discuss and plan. And they might as well start experiencing what life together might mean.

Or so the pastor part of his brain told him, the part that activated a few brain cells during the moments when Edward wasn't reliving the touch.

The touch, now "the feel" in Edward's nomenclature, was more than he had expected.

Playful.

Lustful.

And from Joe.

He could start to see how Kenny would have gotten wrapped up in that lubricating energy. And maybe why Kenny would have run away when it was denied him.

"The feel" unsettled him still, even as Edward worked mindlessly in the kitchen. It had a visceral impact, as his seminary professors would have described it, something that now rummaged about in his gut as he prepared dinner.

Suddenly, he sensed a presence behind him. Joe's hands reached around his torso and clasped together in front. Edward felt Joe's head rest upon his shoulders.

They stood quietly, swayed.

But the peacefulness of that unexpected moment shattered when Edward's phone rang with an entrance request from the main gate.

He turned, kissed Joe's forehead—a strip of skin that seemed so appealing right then—and reached for the phone.

"It was Oscar," Edward said, resting the phone back on its base. Joe had released him and was now merely smiling, a goofy smile, a teenager's smile. Or, as an observer might say, Edward thought in a flash, the smile of a person discovering a new love.

Then the practical Edward reappeared and he said, "I'll have to eat and run. The support group at St. Paul's is tonight, and I've got to set up. But thanks for the hug."

"Anytime," Joe said and winked.

Edward had no words now. He simply nodded and turned back to the stove, concentrating on putting the garlic and ginger into the wok. Joe had moved toward the door to greet Oscar.

Then Edward remembered! He hadn't talked to Joe about Kenny. Joe didn't know Kenny was in his HIV support group. This sharp realization made Edward lose concentration. Maybe he needed to excuse himself from the group, except that his expertise in HIV was one of the reasons St. Paul's vestry and staff were interested in him.

Damn! Edward sighed and, focusing again, added the chicken to the wok. The situation with Kenny wouldn't be such an issue if Edward wasn't in love with Joe. But he was—and becoming more so.

* * *

Edward arrived at St. Paul in the Desert later than usual, leaving him about only ten minutes of setup time. He didn't like being rushed before sessions, but dinner had been so enjoyable. The chatter around the table was about the day; they even laughed at the "flight from Kenny," mercifully initiated by Joe. Actual laughter. That was a good turn of events, providing Edward an optimistic spin on their future relations but keeping him longer than he had planned.

Now he was sprinting from his car to the support group's tidy room and unlocking it. He had brought two six-packs of water, a normal nicety in the desert. He turned on the fans and felt that the room was cool enough to go without air conditioning. Next, he placed the chairs in a circle, counting out the same number of seats as last week, plus one for Kenny and two extra in case someone new showed up.

And then he had a few moments to think about Kenny. Kenny and he had planned to meet separately afterward. They'd probably go over to John's and grab a late-night smoothie. They could talk about Kenny's diagnosis. Talk about his life now. And about Joe? Edward didn't know how to handle that delicate state of play. The pressure of this uncertainty was starting to build up inside again, causing him to fear he'd make some mistake and might raze something dear.

Then Edward heard Kenny's voice, and his heart started to sprint as he turned toward the door.

"Hey, Father," Kenny said, sounding carefree and cheerful.

"Hey," Edward said, almost regretting that he sounded a little breathy. Kenny was a doll, no doubt, but Edward twitched from the pressure. "Did you have a good drive from San Diego?"

Why did he start with a lie? He knew Kenny was at Cy's.

Kenny laughed.

"I've been in town. We are staying at a gay guesthouse. Casa Vista Oro."

Edward exhaled, looking down, sad that he was starting this session with so many cards hidden.

"I know you've been in town. It's awkward," Edward said, rocking on his feet. "I'm a friend of Joe's. From back home." Edward slipped his hands into the front pockets of his shorts and played with his keys. "If that makes you uncomfortable, I'll understand if you want to cancel our meeting." Then he grinned, "It makes me uncomfortable. There are all sorts of boundaries here. Private sharing that I can't go into. You understand?"

Kenny waited a second to respond. "I do. I think I do," Kenny said. He sounded rested, in a better place about this than Edward anticipated. "I'd still like to talk to you after tonight's session." Kenny gestured, pointing to both Edward and himself, and said, "This might be a good thing."

Kenny didn't mind taking an evening jaunt to John's Restaurant after the meeting. They decided to walk over and leave the vehicles in the parish's parking lot.

"You seem better tonight," Edward said after they had settled at a table near the windows with their smoothies. The restaurant was nearly deserted, so there was no need to whisper or invite Kenny outside.

"I've had a great time here with my boyfriend, so it's put me in a good mood. This guesthouse is amazing!" Kenny paused, sipping the smoothie. "And Joe suddenly disappearing from the guesthouse—well, it just seems a little comic to me right now. Shouldn't it? It just shows how much baggage Joe is lugging around." Kenny paused. "But it's his baggage, not mine. His fears, not mine. His anger, not mine. I'm getting clearer about all that. My boyfriend is helping me put it all in perspective."

So, Edward thought, Kenny seems to have gotten over any pressing remorse or uncertainty or discomfort he felt from the Joe separation. Was there something healing in seeing Joe in freefall? Did that view seal the separation between the two men?

Edward kept smiling with his head slightly tilted, but inside he was fighting the urge to explain Joe.

Or, maybe, to discuss Kenny's boyfriend.

Jasper seemed to have become not only boyfriend but therapist. Oh well, this role assumption happened in clergy relationships too. Sometimes it worked out okay. At least it seemed to be working for Kenny.

Kenny smiled briefly and looked at the door. Edward knew he was getting ready to leave. They hadn't discussed Kenny's HIV diagnosis at all. The young man didn't appear to care tonight. Everything seemed rosy for him as they lounged in John's and watched traffic pass on Palm Canyon. Why should Edward disturb that peace? Kenny had his number if the clouds of gloom moved back in.

* * *

Joe sat outside in the condo's walled patio. It was a perfect night, still warm, and far from the downtown bustle and noise. For once, he wasn't mulling about his fickle and erratic fate, having immersed himself into a state of tranquility. His reflections led him to debate whether this new reality of his was womblike, feeling ensconced as he did in the protective walls that Edward and Oscar were helping to build. And the caress of the cooling dry night air was his amniotic fluid.

Then Oscar showed up, and Joe's thoughts began to scramble.

Oscar had gone off to bring his healing hands to a client who, as Oscar had explained, declared himself comfortable only with Oscar— the young stud who didn't lecture him about getting in better shape, losing fat, or gaining muscle.

"That was quick," Joe said softly.

"He wasn't in a good mood," Oscar replied.

Joe let the conversation stall. He sat quietly, eyeing Oscar up and down. Oscar was in running shorts, a fading red string tank top, flip-flops, and had his backpack stuffed with supplies for the night. And there was his smile, beaming even in the dim light of the one electric candle that flickered on the glass-topped table. Joe couldn't get enough of it.

Oscar was facing Joe. He looked up at the moon, placed his hands on his thin hips, and stretched back.

Joe watched him unbend slowly and watched the slight pulse in Oscar's crotch.

Neither of them spoke.

Everything was visual now. Words were packaged up and on the shelf. Communication was in the eyes and in subtle movements, the pitching of shoulders and the rising of chests. Then Oscar knelt in front of Joe, placing both hands on Joe's hairy thighs. With the softest touch, he moved his hands up and down through that patch of hair.

Joe didn't resist. He was floating in the fluid of this womb, now a warm liquid of care and desire. He had wanted this to happen for so many weeks. Now, it seemed to him, was the right time to grab ahold of this desire and steer it forward.

Joe was in a sleep trance. He might have been aware of Oscar standing naked in the guest bedroom, where the two of them had ended up after their patio touching made them seek a flatter, more welcoming surface.

Joe's eyes remained shut, but he was starting to notice the chlorine-rich smell of cum that now permeated the closed-up room. He was waking up slowly from the daze of love. Reason started to take over.

Then it hit him.

What had they done?!

His eyes shot open.

He sat up and shifted his legs over the side of the bed, nearly swatting Oscar, who was eyeing his quick movement with a worried curiosity.

Joe was fully awake. His mind had begun to spin with questions. This wild throw-down with Oscar, a fantasy come true, was it appropriate?

In Edward's space? In Edward's welcoming home?

Oscar was looking at him with that quizzical yet knowing look. "You can't just be, can you?" Oscar asked.

"I'm sorry," Joe said, wincing as he spoke the words, sorry to have withdrawn into his pastor's quiet study. "I love what we did, but I don't know how it fits in. You know, fits into the relationship we're trying to build, you and me and Edward."

Oscar slowly shook his head as if Joe had said enough on that topic. He stood still for a moment, then announced: "Edward will be home soon, but I have to go see my final client. I'm going to clean up."

Joe opened his mouth, but nothing came out, not even the further apologies and explanations that burbled inside.

Oscar picked up his backpack and headed out to the hallway bathroom, turning around to face Joe as he was about to exit. "It's not a disaster. You wait and see."

* * *

Edward found a note on the table when he got home, a slip of lined yellow paper anchored under a single green depression-ware candlestick. It was from Joe and said that he had gone to sleep in the guest bedroom and was sorry he had missed Edward. And Oscar had been called away by another client and might return. Or might not.

Reading the note, Edward felt an irritating dryness in his mouth. Part dehydration and part disappointment.

Edward had wanted to see Joe tonight. To talk about the day they'd had. To wish him a good rest, to hug him tight, and to look into his eyes. And, to be honest, Edward had hoped Oscar would still be there with his verve and his insights. But the young man was off with one of his clients. Maybe he'd return later. Oscar now had the main gate code. Edward raised an eyebrow; that was against association regulations. Oh well, they'd probably move soon.

Edward decided he wouldn't wait up. He took the note and scribbled his own words at the bottom: "I've gone to bed too. See you all in the morning. Or whoever's here." He put the time at the end of the note. If Oscar came home and read it, he'd know when Edward had gone to bed. Or maybe Joe would get up in the middle of the night...

Edward went over to the sofa and fluffed the cushions. They'd have to figure out how sleeping would happen. But Oscar was a young man, supple and pliant, with few pretensions. That upbeat attitude was one of the things Edward had liked about Oscar right from the start.

Moving toward his room, Edward tried to be quiet so he wouldn't disturb Joe. He stopped a second at the guest bedroom door, stared at the doorknob, and tugged at his t-shirt collar suddenly feeling the evening's heat that still clung in the hallway.

Edward knit his eyebrows, wrinkled his forehead, and stood still.

He remembered Joe's freedom at the pool, chatting and joking and taking a drag of weed. And that moment in the water. This afternoon. That touch.

His hand moved to knock on the guest bedroom door, but he turned away, exhaling his sadness. Or frustration. He felt the need so strongly tonight. It made him grit his teeth.

Edward reached his bed at last, dropping his clothes on the floor and leaving them. He was tired, and the day's tensions and desires quickly faded away in the quiet desert night, and sleep came easily.

Edward wasn't sure if he was dreaming, if the touch was a blurred and scratchy fantasy wish come true or something else. His mind was trying to form the name, his go-to name for fantasy. Joe. He shifted over in the bed, barely aware. It was his natural response when someone else climbed in. After so many years with his wife, he knew the drill. But now...

He was waking, rising more from the deep, not wanting to open his eyes though. He raised himself, inhaled, and brought his soul more into consciousness. He forced his eyes open, left then right. And what he saw, once the blurriness faded, was a naked Oscar next to him with his animal-charm smile. All silent. The clear, active eyes of a young man at the prime of life.

Edward's breathing became shallower as his body reacted. Not Joe. Oscar. Hot, kind Oscar. Of course he needed a place to sleep. He was tired of couch surfing.

The young man raised an arm and gently drew it down Edward's chest. Edward tensed.

Oscar sensed Edward's hesitancy; he must have, the wise young man. The young man who knew the wavering fears of older men. He put a finger on Edward's lips and shook his head, a signal Edward took to mean "Be quiet." Or "Submit."

So Edward released the tension in his back. He closed his eyes.

Oscar's hands were slow and constant. Moving up and down his chest. Each time edging lower.

And lower.

And Edward responded. He kept his eyes shut. He had become a teen having a wet dream, strong and undiluted. Could this be?

Edward woke in peace. It was early, and Oscar was still there, breathing calmly, a low hum.

As his mind began to clear, he realized he had awakened without a thought of Joe.

But the name, now speeding down his synapses, jolted Edward.

How would this be explained?

Damn! He didn't want to ruin the blissful moment.

Edward began to stir, as did Oscar.

And Edward watched as the naked form next to him emerged from a cluster of pillows and sheets and tossed-off clothing.

"Good morning," Oscar said, more to the pillow than to Edward. He flipped over and rubbed his eyes.

Edward could see all of Oscar now. The ripple of young-man muscles, the tufts of hair from armpits and groin, the young-man cock that was enlarging slightly, then softening again.

"I don't want to do anything this morning," Oscar said, moving to cover himself. "I like to save myself for when I'm more attentive."

"Oh...fine," Edward said, surprised, amused, almost laughing. He was expecting nothing more, that last night was a one-off. But Oscar sounded as if he expected something more.

"What do we tell Joe?" Edward blurted out. His anxiety was mounting now, fueled by a fear of driving away an impulsive Joe.

"I'll tell him," Oscar said. "Later."

The young man got off the bed and began putting on last night's clothes.

"Then I'll start breakfast," Edward said, also getting out of bed.

Oscar stood there, observing, while Edward quickly dressed. A t-shirt, shorts, and sandals.

Oscar winked, turned toward the door, and opened it. He stuck out his head to look down the hall.

Oscar turned back and shook his head, which Edward assumed meant that Joe's door was closed. Then he left.

Edward wasn't surprised that Joe was still asleep. Joe needed sleep more than they did. He had pulsed with energy yesterday, surely burning through most of his reserve, imagining a future in Palm Springs that was similar to his past.

Edward followed Oscar but stopped in the kitchen. It was nearly five o'clock, and he could see some of the residents of the condo association were already out walking their dogs or getting in their morning exercise.

Oscar stood on the patio in his shorts, stretching. "I'm going for a swim," he said, his voice loud enough to reach inside. "You want to join?"

Edward was already sorting through the contents of the refrigerator, thinking that a jaunt to Ralphs was necessary. But he turned toward Oscar and said, "Sure. Fine idea."

They both padded quietly back to the bedroom to change.

"Do you have trunks with you?" Edward asked.

"Yes, but in my bag out front. I'm sure they could use a wash. Can I borrow a pair of yours?" Oscar answered, placing his hands around Edward's slim waist. "I think they'd fit me."

Edward closed his eyes. This was so nice. And so chancy. Joe was just down the hall. How could he be doing this? He lacked an explanation.

"Don't worry," Oscar said, piercing Edward's worrying thoughts with his easygoing mantra. "It'll be okay. I have this sense."

The pool was empty except for them. They both did laps and chatted in between. Nothing serious. This was morning exercise.

Then Joe showed up, not in trunks, but in his old work clothes. "Hey, you guys left me!" Joe was smiling, but Edward thought he sensed a rebuke—a small boy telling his pals to include him.

"We're getting our exercise," Oscar answered, looking up from the shallow end of the pool. "You were sleeping like a baby when we left. You can still get in." Oscar made a grand gesture, inviting Joe into the open pool.

Edward watched this exchange with a certain detachment. He thought he saw the tenseness in Joe's shoulders relax. Of course, the magic of Oscar. The power of his appeal and his sweetness.

"I've got to run," Joe said, glancing at his watch and shifting his feet. "I was thinking about what I'm going to do and decided to see Luis instead of staying away another day. Get an idea how things are at Casa Vista Oro. Talk about my employment status. Go to work if I still have a job."

Joe had spoken to Oscar but, then, he looked at Edward. "Do you think that's a good idea?"

Edward tried to look serious. This was the Joe he wanted, the guy who acted. "Talk is always good. And Luis is a friend of yours. He's a friend of Cy's, too, so don't give away too much."

Joe smiled and chortled. "It's like a soap opera, no?"

"I'll be around all day," Edward said. "Only a couple of errands to run. You'll be back?"

Joe put his hands in his pants, looking at Edward and, then, at Oscar. "I'll be back after work, barring the unforeseen. You guys enjoy yourselves. It's going to be a nice day."

Edward and Oscar both stood in the pool and watched Joe hurry away, down the path that would take him back to the condo.

They kept watching him until he turned the corner and was out of sight. Then they looked at each other.

Edward waited for Oscar to speak. He began to feel bleak because of Joe's burden, which he felt he shared. And he couldn't stop worrying about how Joe would take this new development with Oscar.

"I've seen those eyes before," Oscar said. "There's a cloud covering your blue beauties."

Edward moved a little closer. "My gut is a war zone, and my head is definitely clouded. I'm full of fear, or anxiety, Oscar. Full of it."

"You don't want to lose him because of what we did," Oscar said, facing Edward fully. "I don't either. But I like you, Edward. And what we did felt right, no? I'm sure you agree or will in time."

* * *

Joe drove a little faster than normal, wanting to catch Luis at the apartment before his roommate headed to Casa Vista Oro. Joe thought he might be too late and would have to call Luis and meet him for lunch. He needed to know where things stood with Cy. And whether Kenny and Jasper were still there.

Chapter 20

Luis's truck was outside, parked on the street, ready for him to drive off. Luis could have walked to work, but Joe was sure his roommate was waiting for him upstairs.

Joe realized he was coming with both a head full of new ideas and a hesitancy to share them, even with Luis who had been kind to him.

Joe was sure Cy had encouraged Luis to gather as much information as possible.

Then Joe laughed, delighted by the thought of his new household, a group of men who were opening up to each other. Such a contrast to Luis's household!

Joe walked right in without pausing, correctly assuming the door was unlocked. Luis was at the table, sitting in meditation with a cup of coffee, a scrap of paper, and a pencil at its side.

Joe stopped a few feet from Luis and looked around, recalling how recently he had come here in his exile, or should he say "Kenny infatuation," or simply "HIV panic." And how he now had a new perspective. It felt good, and a smile blossomed.

"Luis, thanks for hanging around so we could talk," Joe said even before he sat.

Luis nodded. "There's coffee if you want it," he said, gesturing to the Formica counter and the 10-cup Mr. Coffee. "It's fresh," Luis added with a grin.

Joe realized how well Luis had come to know him. The outside things anyway.

Joe poured coffee into one of the mugs that Cy had given them. A full dozen from the gay men's chorus. Cy had tendrils everywhere.

Joe stood briefly at the window and looked out at the empty pool. None of the regulars were up for their morning swim. It was early here at the complex, whose residents were chiefly slow risers on limited incomes, or some very depressed and disabled, or others no longer concerned about a lazy morning. Cy's wards, in truth. Cy wasn't a totally bad man, but his flaws could wound those near him.

"Luis, you've been good to me," Joe said, sitting down. He placed the coffee mug on the table and circled its rim with his right index finger.

He was still working out what else to say when Luis asked, "Are you planning on leaving?"

A note of sadness sounded in that question, which surprised Joe and made him worry whether he might be doing some harm.

"Eventually, yes. The timeline is unclear."

Luis pushed away his coffee cup. He was unsettled, not his normal self.

"Have you spoken to Cy about me? About my situation?" Joe asked.

He had to wait a moment for Luis to deliver his answer.

"You have learned some of his faults, certainly," Luis began, shifting slightly in his chair. "And you are a priest—a man of faults who deals with men of faults. No?"

Joe took a sip of coffee. *So it comes back to that*, he thought. Why bring up his priesthood now? Was Luis angry or annoyed because Joe had given up a highly respectable job?

Joe set his coffee cup down. "I am a man of faults," he finally said, wary and waiting.

Luis looked up at the ceiling for a moment, then directly at Joe. "I am not your enemy. I hope you know that. But there are lines and allegiances. Lifelines, you might say. I need to hold onto mine."

Joe breathed in, picking up the strong smell of immigrant fear.

"So...am I welcomed back to work? Am I to leave this apartment immediately?"

Now the answer was swift. "He'd prefer the two weeks' notice. Everything on the up-and-up. No scandal. No rumors. Your choice when to leave."

Joe sat still, his heart beating strong and regular. Oddly, he was very calm. This was it. The ultimatum—but not so terrible.

"You're a good man, Luis," Joe said, as he rose to go change into fresh work clothes, suddenly remembering that he needed to take his daily meds. Luckily, he kept a stash at Luis's for safety reasons.

Luis got up also and stopped to look steadily into Joe's eyes. After a moment, he put a hand on Joe's shoulder. "You're a good man too, Joe. Don't let this..." Luis didn't seem to know the word. He smiled, "... *fracaso* stop you. Keep going. Please. Keep going."

Luis's encouragement cracked Joe's resolve to share little.

He wanted to share his plan.

"I have a goal now: to establish a home for homeless LGBT teens. The three of us will be working on it, have been working on it. So I will keep going. Doing good, I hope."

Luis shot Joe an instant, satisfied smile and moved to put his cup in the sink, then headed for the door. "Oh, by the way," he said, turning around, "the San Diegans were leaving before dawn."

And then he was out.

* * *

At the guesthouse, Joe was assigned to clean Kenny and Jasper's room. He expected that it was a punishment of some kind, at least in Cy's mind, but he was happy to get back to work, and a room was a room. Besides, his thoughts were bending elsewhere.

When he was about to empty the wastebasket in the living room, Joe noticed a religious pamphlet. A brochure for activities and groups rather than fundamentalist bold-faced quotes—the "magic spells" he used to call them when he was cynical about his calling.

Joe looked over his shoulder, to make sure he wasn't being watched, and took the brochure into the bathroom to read. He shut the door for privacy and leaned back against the vanity. The brochure had been folded, maybe carried in a back pants pocket, retained as an object of some value. One thing stood out. An activity was circled. The HIV support group.

Edward's group.

Kenny had been in Edward's group.

Joe felt hollow and kept staring at the brochure. It was a connection Joe hadn't anticipated. Not that it was bad. He had loved Kenny. He loved Edward. And Kenny was reaching out. Who could deny him help?

It was just that. Kenny was reaching out to someone else. Joe was no longer that ready source of comfort.

* * *

Kenny felt a kind of release as he parked his F-150 at his apartment complex. Release. That's the only word he could think of. Like a wounded raptor back home he'd seen released from a cage that flew up and away without a glance back.

That's how Kenny felt as he stepped out of his truck and began walking to his apartment. He didn't know why he felt the sense of release, but he thought Jasper was feeling a similar, new emotion.

Their last love-making at the guesthouse had been calmer and quieter, like two men with a solid connection, a bond. Something with a long future.

Jasper had kissed him at the front door of his apartment as Kenny was leaving. Jasper had never kissed Kenny outside at his apartment complex, a place crammed with Marine and support staff families.

Jasper was definitely feeling something too, Kenny thought. Fearlessness, on top of a certainty.

* * *

Cy had watched Joe head to Kenny and Jasper's suite to clean and sighed while watching, not out of longing but as an expression of frustration. This was a man he had wanted to help. He had helped. And now?

Cy kept his eyes trained on the doorway Joe had entered. Not to time Joe's work but to reflect.

A friend of Cy's was coming to town to shoot a film. An internet porno. What if Cy could dangle a porno role in front of Joe? Would he do it for the money? He would need money to fund his plans. Yes, Luis had told Cy about Joe's dream of creating a place for homeless gay youth. The porno film would cause conflict inside him for sure. What would the priest say to it? Would he sell himself for thirty pieces of silver? Would he see the film as a practical move to achieve a higher goal?

Cy recognized this was a fanciful plan. What were its odds of success? Still, He couldn't forget the hot coil inside men, especially the poorly formed, that made them do desperate things. If Joe signed on to do the porno, he might begin to break down.

Not that Cy wanted to destroy anyone, but Joe's liaison with Oscar competed with Cy's plans for the lovable, hot *Latino*. He had the right to act.

* * *

Joe drove back to Luis's apartment after work, having spent most of the day on autopilot. He had zoned out trying to keep the feeling of rejection that flooded him after seeing the flyer in Kenny's room from ruining his mood. As he approached the apartment, his mood lifted and he began to flit through images of the last days, quietly telling himself stories about his new life. He replayed the images of the happy trio living and working together, cooking and eating leisurely meals, hanging by the pool, making plans to help homeless gay youth.

After arriving, he only wanted to clean up, then start to sort through items that could be packed early: his few books, CDs, photos, winter clothes. He heard Luis in the kitchen, probably getting ready to make dinner.

"Are you eating here tonight?" Luis called out.

"Just a sec and I'll let you know," Joe called back, feeling like a moocher. Luis was nothing but generous with his time and efforts. But Joe wanted to talk to Edward. Without Oscar around.

He made a quick call. "Hey, I'm back from work. Do you have any dinner plans?"

"No," Edward said, his voice bright.

Joe picked up a photo of Edward and himself from back home, studying it as he listened to Edward.

"I'm in the kitchen reviewing what's in the fridge and cupboards." Edward paused. "Do you want to come over and help out?"

"Yes. I'm just packing up some items here, then I'll head over. I suppose Oscar is with a client."

"That's true. The guy is booked these days!"

"It'll just be us," Joe said, hearing in his voice the relief and wondering why he needed to be so worried. Whatever they would say to each other would eventually get said to Oscar. Still, he wanted this to be personal.

Joe felt a nagging itch to speak about Kenny.

* * *

Joe parked his car and got out, hefting the backpack filled with what he needed for tomorrow morning and the following day. Picking up that bundle jabbed him unexpectedly with concern. He was now moving into someone else's life without having all the boundaries described and set, the contracts reviewed and signed.

He stopped a second and looked around at the condo association grounds and the patios that opened onto them. By moving forward tonight, he supposed, he was making a commitment. A commitment to Edward and to Oscar. To the three of them.

Over the last days, Oscar had repeatedly assured him that guys in Palm Springs do this all the time. They form households.

But he had never done anything like this before, old as he was. He'd lived at the seminary and then gone to live where the diocese sent him, primarily at Mater Dei. He'd never reached out to others, especially guys he wanted to hang with, in order to form his own community. Their own community.

He felt so unprepared.

Yet he had this feeling, like a premonition.

And the premonition got stronger as he stood there, sending a shiver up his body, something that quivered inside him like a child's anticipation of a holiday surprise.

He took a deep breath and looked forward.

Edward was at the patio's gate, waiting for him, dressed in a white guayabera shirt and white shorts. His skin had darkened, and with a full head of soft gray hair and sky blue eyes that shone with the gleam of gems in the light, he looked like a model for a leisure magazine.

Joe called out as he neared the patio's gate, "I'm prepared to stay the night if we get on a roll in our planning." Edward moved out into the sun, which illuminated the white and gray and dazzling eyes and limber stride, and Joe stopped. Why had he not seen this before? Studied it. The appeal of this man.

"Anything wrong at the apartment?" Edward asked as he opened the gate. Joe smiled. Edward probably thought there might have been another Cy intervention.

Joe set his bags down and looked into Edward's eyes. "I'm just so happy you're in my life." Then they hugged. Not an overlong hug, but something tipping over the walled edge of friendship. Joe was the first to release. But he didn't start to walk away. He stayed and stared into Edward's eyes.

"You're welcome here, Joe," Edward said, "very welcome." Edward's hands were at his sides, but Joe could sense the desire. It centered between them.

Joe smiled at Edward, pointed his head toward the condo's door, and moved to go inside.

Dinner had been quick. A glass of wine and a stir-fry. They had a frozen yogurt out in the front patio, washed up the dishes, and went for a walk around the compound.

It was a peaceful night. Joe was feeling content.

They didn't hold hands, but Joe noticed Edward seemed to bump into him every so often. Not that Joe minded.

Over dinner they had discussed contacting a realtor but would wait for Oscar's advice. They'd look at houses near or in Cathedral City, somewhere not so fancy where they'd have to keep up the appearances for tourists. They could start there with the three of them. See how it went.

"I'll need another job, so I can give two weeks' notice," Joe said as they ambled past pool 3 and its guardian ficus trees.

"Is there anything you won't consider?" Edward asked, stopping to gaze up at the mountain.

Joe laughed. "Nothing sexual."

Edward put his arm on Joe's shoulder. "Don't worry; we won't prostitute you."

They had looped around the entire compound and were returning to Edward's condo. Joe was thinking how grateful he was that, at least, they had this place. It would be his refuge in a few days. He took a moment to study Edward's beautiful face that was now lit by a nearby streetlamp.

But, as they neared the condo's patio gate, Joe became anxious again about the topic of Kenny. He'd been putting it off all night. What to say?

"Should we sit out here a while?" Joe asked, needing to be done with the topic of his ex. They had entered into the condo's front patio. Joe sat down in a plastic chair at the small table, the whole of it still warm from the day's exposure. He said, "Just a few minutes. I have something I want to talk about."

This announcement stopped Edward, who had been walking toward the condo door. He turned back.

Edward's face was partly in shadow but lit enough for Joe to make out his features: the long nose and well-set eyes, the wave of gray hair bordering his forehead and drifting down, the wide mouth that was now searching for a smile. Joe finally was seeing Edward the way others saw him. He wasn't sure why. But this was his Edward.

He sat and waited for Edward to sit down.

"Thank you," Joe said as Edward pulled up another chair, moving close to him.

Joe reached out his right hand and placed it above Edward's knee, feeling, maybe for the first time, the light fuzz that covered Edward's thigh.

Instead of speaking, he only rubbed Edward's thigh a while. He knew he was being forward, but he didn't care. Not tonight. Not in this evening's dusk as the mountain's outline darkened further and began to disappear.

Edward's gaze was on him. Joe knew he had to get out some words. On topic. About Kenny. *Tell it how it was,* he reminded himself. Joe withdrew his hand and coughed to clear the lump from his throat.

"I was cleaning Kenny's guest suite at Casa Vista Oro," Joe said, finally beginning. He reached into his back pocket and pulled out the folded brochure. Its writing looked faded in the evening dimness, but the boldly printed "HIV" still stood out.

Edward held his head steady. "You cleaned their room. Of course."

There was a quiet in his voice and something cool, something nervous.

"I had to tell you," Joe said. "I'm not sure why anymore. Why it makes a difference. Except that finding this brochure shocked me and dulled my spirit. It made me feel unwanted and, at the same time, uncaring."

Joe stopped.

Edward seemed to dig inside himself for the right response. Finally, he said, "Kenny is still new to the diagnosis. And he's also entering into a new relationship. Two big changes in his life. Of course, you know it can help to talk these things out. It can change the dynamic, no?" Edward shifted slightly. "And this group appealed to him, maybe because it was away from San Diego, maybe because it was church-based. I don't really know." Edward looked down. "It makes me uncomfortable talking about this. I'm sure you understand. Maybe I should have told you before. Maybe I shouldn't lead that group."

Joe shook his head vigorously, yet said nothing for a few seconds. His response came easily. "See him all you want, Edward. I'm sure you can help him. That's all I wanted to say."

Now Joe simply gazed at Edward, who was looking back with his kind eyes.

Joe settled back into his chair, feeling more relaxed, he thought, than he had in months.

"I'm here for you, Joe," Edward said quietly after a while, "just as I'm here for Kenny. But I'm here for you in a different way." Then

Edward extended a hand to Joe as if to help him up. Joe took Edward's hand and rose.

Together they walked into the house, holding hands. Both were clasping tight, Joe feeling—and liking—the roughness of his hand in comparison to Edward's.

Even as Edward turned to lock the front door, Joe held on. Edward grinned at Joe, his face part impish, part wise.

And so it went. Joe walked silently and willingly with Edward back to his friend's bedroom. Edward closed the bedroom door, then came back to stand in front of Joe. Their eyes locked a few minutes, but Joe didn't mind. Everything inside him was still. His mind had quieted. He needed this.

First the kissing, slow and deep. No words were spoken.

And then the undressing.

And now he was waking up in Edward's bed, feeling relaxed. So unexpected, as if he'd discovered a missing part of himself. Joe lay in bed and remembered the kissing, the heat that remained after they'd already both come. Then the relaxation, Edward asking if the overhead fan bothered him, Joe saying it didn't. They had been so at ease.

His friend was still sleeping, one hand settled next to Joe's naked side.

Joe was thirsty and needed to pee. He glanced at the alarm clock. It was one thirty. He moved slowly, rolling to the side, using his core to flex himself up.

Joe decided to go to the hall bathroom, hoping that distant flushing sound wouldn't wake Edward. He opened the bedroom door with a silent turn of the knob, stepped out, and pulled the door shut.

Joe stood a moment looking at the door, wondering now, as his brain became more awake, how he'd explain the evening's doings to Oscar. It needed an explanation, no? Didn't he and Oscar have a burgeoning relationship? One of trust, openness, touch?

And so it was with a jolt that he turned quickly around when he felt a touch on his ass.

Joe almost gasped, startled as he was in the quiet hallway.

There was Oscar. Naked.

Oscar turned Joe fully around and leaned to whisper into his ear, "Good morning."

Then he knelt and took Joe into his mouth. Oscar raised his hands up to Joe's nipples and torqued them softly in unison with the movement of his head.

Joe was off the charts. All the books on love and relationships and moral boundaries had shut tight. Joe placed his hands on Oscar's head and ran his fingers through Oscar's tight curls. He contracted his stomach, pulling in his abs. All this was so amazing.

He let his mind's patter stall in the bliss of this moment.

And soon he came again. His breath became ragged and his eyes rolled in their sockets.

A moment later Oscar rose, and they both hugged.

Joe was finally able to pee. Alone in the hallway bathroom after he'd jerked off Oscar.

There was a smile on Joe's face. A smile of accomplishment, the way he used to grin after he'd preached a sermon with depth and dramatic turns.

And this, this entire evening, was a dramatic turn all right. He hadn't even seen the bend before he was in it, but he'd taken the curve with all the skill he possessed, feeling the pull of a force that he had avoided for so long, giving in to it now as he navigated into the curve.

And out of it.

Joe was quieting down. He wiped himself off.

And now what?

He paused to examine himself in the mirror. He was naked still. In someone else's house. With two men who had come into his life just when he needed them. Together they had offered him a way forward in this gated desert landscape.

And now he'd had sex with both of them. Something he'd done with relish. There was a fervor in his attraction to both. He could still remember their smells. One older and thicker, the other sharper and more vivid.

Joe looked at his eyes, trying to see if the guilt he anticipated was reflected there. He only saw the glistening of satisfaction.

His smile deepened and he breathed in and out, long breaths. Everything was going to be all right, maybe. He breathed deeply again. Thinking of the next steps. He needed to talk with Edward and Oscar together.

Didn't he?

He returned to Edward's bed, which now also hosted Oscar. He got little sleep and woke again at four thirty to the sound of movement in the condo.

Both Oscar and Edward were in the kitchen with all the lights blazing when Joe, now dressed in running pants and a sleeveless t-shirt, entered. Edward was making coffee, and Oscar had started on a large frittata, cutting an onion and cracking eggs with swift aplomb.

"Can you make toast? We've decided on an early breakfast. Really early! There's so much energy in this house!" Oscar said, turning back to look at Joe, flashing him a smile with a playful head tilt.

Edward also turned, locking eyes with Joe, sending him a wry smile that radiated a comfort that Joe hadn't noticed previously.

Joe began to butter the first of the toast. He was happy to have something to concentrate on. They all did, he was sure. Both of his friends' heads had to be buzzing as loudly as his. What were they all up to?

They were all seated, their plates loaded up like the threesome were athletes preparing for a long slog on the field.

Edward was at the head of the table, which seemed appropriate to Joe. Edward reached his hands out, moments after sitting down and before any more chatter might start. Joe and Oscar reached out to Edward to take a hand, then reached across the table to hold each other's. "Let's calm our souls," Edward said, "call ourselves to attention." Then he closed his eyes and bowed his head. Joe watched him carefully, looking at Edward's eyelashes and the tangle of hair that had fallen over his forehead. Then he looked over at Oscar who was deep in concentration, his subtle chest movement, peaceful and regular, seen through the tight white t-shirt.

Then Edward gripped firmly and released Joe's and Oscar's hands. "Let's eat," Edward said, picking up his fork.

"Oops, I forgot...pills" Joe said, pushing back his chair and hurrying to Edward's bedroom where his overnight bag had finally landed. He took his pillbox into the bathroom. He hated forgetting this routine but understood the need for the constant supply of their protecting compounds in his body. He wasn't a neophyte anymore, but he still lapsed into old habits.

Joe returned to the table without a smile on his face. He knew his frustration with his health was curling his lips and making him frown. And he was preoccupied now. He had to get off to work soon. He still had a job. He didn't want to leave Cy with any excuse to berate him.

"Sorry, guys," Joe said as he settled down. "I've got to get to work soon, so if anyone wants to talk about last night, we'd better get at it."

Edward and Oscar both looked at Joe, then looked away. Joe's words and brusque tone had seemed like a challenge.

"Let's talk later," Edward said, breaking an uncomfortable silence. "I sometimes forget I'm the only one with only a single commitment every week."

Silence again.

"Last night was good," Edward said. "I have to say that." He turned his head to look at Joe as if he were expecting a response.

So there it was, the moment of truth. And Joe had yet to marshal a clear thought.

Then Oscar coughed so that both Joe and Edward looked at him. "I think, right now, we're building something. And it's fragile. But to be honest..." Oscar paused, looking separately at each of them, "we're building something I desire."

Chapter 21

Joe hustled in through the guesthouse's side gate, throwing a glance at the office window and Cy, who sat at his desk concentrating on his computer. Cy didn't look up. He wore his telephone headset, probably talking to a new guest asking for dates or making other trip inquiries.

Joe checked his watch. He was a minute late, but who could complain? Luis would give him that enigmatic smile, and Cy would probably shrug off the missing minute. Still, Joe rushed to get on with the day's work.

Several couples had already gathered at the breakfast nook. Midwesterners, Joe assumed. People like him, or like how he used to be, well rested and ready for the day. Now he'd arrived late, having spent his free time in a sexual frenzy. Or so last night seemed. It was the memory of bodies that most obsessed him. He had fallen into a pit of flesh and had enjoyed every second of it.

* * *

Edward was busy cleaning dishes as Oscar whisked up crumbs from the table. Next, Oscar helped dry the dishes and put them away, earning a welcoming smile from Edward. The two of them hadn't said much after Joe's departure. Was Oscar waiting for Joe's return?

"A final cup of coffee?" Oscar asked

"Sure, let's enjoy them on the front patio," Edward said, hoping that he and Oscar might review the night's bedroom intimacies. As he had silently washed up, troubling thoughts began to bother him. They took the form of questions: Was there love in their bed last night? And if so, in what configuration?

Perhaps Joe had been right to want an all-out conversation at breakfast. Edward's new and nagging fear was that last night was only some form of Palm Springs accommodation that held a pale resemblance to love. In truth, he wanted last night and this morning to repeat.

No sooner had Oscar and Edward settled in lounge chairs with their cups of coffee than the next-door neighbor stopped by on his dog walk and offered a morning greeting. They both rose and went to the patio gate, Edward responding with a warm hello.

The three of them chatted briefly about a new restaurant on Date Palm and the prices at Ralphs vs Albertsons. Edward knew the retired insurance man had wanted more interaction because his eyes could barely leave Oscar, moving obviously from head to crotch. He probably would have liked an invitation to a cup of coffee.

"He found you fetching," Edward said as the two of them settled down again to enjoy their now cooling brew.

"He did. And he could be a client," Oscar said.

"You didn't hand him a card?"

"No. I didn't want him to think you had hired me for the night!" Oscar smiled and reached over to hold Edward's hand. "You're in a different category for me."

Edward startled, blushed, and smiled back, pulsing his hold on Oscar's hand.

"Honestly, I don't know how to make sense of it all," Edward said. "What happened these last few days has left me...perplexed." Edward looked over at Oscar, whose eyes had clouded with Edward's use of that inanimate word. "Not bad perplexed! Pleased, or intrigued perplexed, if that makes any sense."

Oscar smiled now. "I like you, Edward Brockton."

Oscar paused a moment, letting the announcement penetrate. "I'm so glad Joe brought us together." He let go of Edward's hand. "You two really complement each other, although I'm not sure Joe sees it. But

I do. Maybe you do too. I see you as the wiser older brother and he as the bewildered younger brother." Oscar shifted in his chair, broadening his smile.

Edward's mind held onto the word "brother," putting it away for later consideration.

Oscar released his hold on Edward's hand, which Edward took as a stopping point. But, then, he spoke again. "You are both attractive—in different ways, obviously. But the real point I want to make is...you are both attractive to me, as friends...and more than friends. Something we experienced fully last night."

Edward shifted his head now, leaning in a bit closer, trying to grasp the heart of Oscar's meaning. Oscar seemed to be describing a group attraction for which Edward had no theological context, and this lack of schooling stuck a burr in his seminary-formed conscience. How could he explain it to friends? Or at St Paul's?

They sat quietly and sipped their coffees.

* * *

Joe went back to the apartment after work and headed directly into his room after greeting Luis. He stopped briefly in his doorway as a strong sense of change overcame him that was part ardor fueled by last night's sex and part nervous excitement standing at the borderland of the unknown.

He showered and changed into clean clothes—shorts and a t-shirt—then made his exit.

"I'll be out tonight for dinner, Luis," Joe said, happily heading to Edward's, where he hoped the door to some novel mansion of love remained unlocked.

When he got to Edward's, he found his friend sitting on the sofa in a darkened living room, no brew or drink at his side, no TV nattering; it was as if Edward waited in a chapel, his soul eager for peace and lucidity.

Joe stopped at the doorway, at first wondering if he'd overstepped his welcome by barging in with his guest key.

After a moment, Edward looked up at him and smiled, but with only a pastor's welcoming smile, lacking the warmth Joe had come to expect. Joe stayed at the doorway. Edward had something on his mind, something concerning.

Edward turned his head slightly and tapped on the spot next to him, saying, "Have a seat."

Joe felt a slight worry press his lips together as he nestled close to Edward. He did not want to begin this talk with an awkward space between them.

"You seemed lost in thought," Joe said as he placed his right hand on Edward's leg, lightly brushing the hair.

Edward startled. "I *was* lost in thought. Lost in thought about what's going on with the three of us."

Joe quickly moved his hand back into his own lap.

"You're concerned. Are you concerned that we're making a mess of a good thing?" Joe asked. That worry had gnawed on Joe during the day, alternating throughout with enticing thoughts of a new life with these two. The three of them had been getting along so well. Would the same magic spell bind them if they moved in together? Slept together?

Edward tilted his head in response to Joe's question. "All three of us have a good thing, I guess, or good separate relationships. But, to be honest, when I think of Oscar—neither of us has spent much time together with him. And you and I have such differences. I'm older than both of you. You and I are classically educated, with years of Latin and wrestling with the works of long-dead church fathers and philoso-phers—a strange education to many."

Joe listened, feeling a chill seep in.

"And we've both borne the yoke of moral authority," Edward said, continuing. "That does something to a person. Makes you careful."

Edward stopped to gaze into Joe's eyes.

Joe had been nodding as he listened to Edward's list of worries, hoping they were only unexpressed concerns that needed to be said then brushed aside. As the day progressed, he had become more con-fident about their future. He was ready to begin constructing this new relationship, even if its shape were fuzzy and its functioning a day-today series of negotiations. But he needed Edward's commitment to charge ahead at full steam.

"I understand your concern," Joe said, trying to cover a slight feeling of disappointment. "We can slow down, I guess, except I'm soon out of a job and a place to stay."

Edward reached over to rub Joe's shoulder. "I know that time is pressuring us," he said. He withdrew his hand. "Not time on some indifferent clock that's ticking down, but Cy. Cy is applying the pressure. On you, which means us."

* * *

Oscar had an evening massage appointment with a guest at Casa Vista Oro. He knew these guest appointments came from Cy's recommendation, a fact that made Oscar nervous tonight with a prickling feeling snaking over his skin.

He was rarely nervous anymore. His life was palatable—even enjoyable at times—happier than his tense, desperate fundamentalist childhood. But he knew that it could all unravel if he angered one of the forces behind his business success, which was how he referred to any stability in his life.

No way to deny it, Cy had been instrumental in furthering his success.

Cy had taught him how to deal with clients who were sophisticated and rungs above him on the social ladder. Cy even taught him how to move a massage to something more. And how to transform an evening's luxury into assisting a poor youth, maybe allowing him to stay over for a night or a week. Cy had taught him how to do it without becoming a gigolo or a leech. Cy knew the boundaries. It was a culture Cy had explored and analyzed. A culture he inhabited.

On this late afternoon, Oscar was about to cross a line. Actually, he'd already crossed it. He'd aligned himself with Joe. Sought him out, cultivated him, and fell for him.

And now, unexpectedly, he'd decided it needed to be the three of them. Only the three of them would truly make Joe whole—make all of them whole—and cement together pieces that had fallen away.

Spirit.

Laughter.

Lust.

And, of course, Love.

So Oscar readied himself, deep inside. A terrain he knew well. He was afraid to lose Cy's approval. And Cy's assistance.

But he was falling deeper in love. He was building up a different kind of relationship, a relationship that wasn't constructed to help keep himself alive and fed and housed. Rather, it was a relationship of attraction.

Joe understood Edward's unease, shared it. The three of them and Oscar's youth.

And Joe knew one thing, garnered from television movies and his own experience: every relationship needed a spark, a chemical ignition.

And Oscar was that spark for him—and for Edward too. Joe knew this truth deep inside him, from head down to toe. It was a living bit of knowledge.

It wasn't a moral argument that was gnawing at Edward's guts. Right? Or maybe it was.

Edward couldn't make a clear assessment of his situation. He had wanted to come to Palm Springs to follow his one love—Joe. Now, if he admitted it beyond the small fairy ring that centered around his heart, he was in love with two men.

He seemed to have entered into another land where six hands linked together made a unity. He shook his head. Joe was on the sofa next to him, resting on his arm, something he'd prayed for on bended knee. Now it was happening, but with this unanticipated codicil: that a relationship with Joe required a relationship with Oscar.

That phrasing had not been used. The rules hadn't been voted on and enacted. The relationship was evolving on its own, a new planting with roots sharing the same soil and feeding off the same nutrients.

Edward inhaled sharply, causing Joe to look up.

"Are you all right?

"Pretty much," Edward answered, which was near to but not quite the truth. "You know Oscar is a delight," he said.

Joe sat up, jerking his head like a man who suddenly wakes up in a new space.

Edward laughed and looked at Joe. "He'll be here soon. I think we need him here. He's our necessary third element."

The doorbell rang—twice, three times—incessant as an alarm. That cute young face had arrived, back from the last client of the day. Finally. Joe felt Oscar's energy already thrum through the quiet room.

Edward got up, lifting himself from the sofa by placing one hand on Joe's leg, turning back slightly and winking at him. "I'll get the door."

Joe turned to watch Oscar's entrance. The young man was carrying his table and all his gear.

"Sorry to disturb, but I couldn't reach my keys while carrying all this stuff," Oscar said, smiling broadly and then planting a kiss on Edward's lips as Edward leaned in to help with the table.

Joe watched carefully, feeling a warm glow of satisfaction as he watched Edward put a hand on Oscar's shoulder to welcome him inside. Post kiss, Edward turned immediately to look at Joe and winked again.

It feels like a signal, Joe thought about the wink as he rose to join them. A signal that fate, or the gods, or a good god was smiling on the three of them.

But where would they get enough cash?

Chapter 22

Someone's phone rang, causing the sleeping pile to stir. It was Joe's phone, and he shunted himself out of bed, offering a soft "Sorry" to Edward and Oscar.

He snatched up the phone and padded out into the hallway, which was dark and quiet. He checked the caller ID. It was Luis. Was Joe late already? It was only four thirty. Had something happened? He pressed the green phone button.

"A heads up," Luis said, speaking softly.

"Are you at home?" Joe asked, trying to clear his mind.

"No. I had to fix a plumbing issue." Luis paused. "I learned something. I wanted to let you know."

Joe was still sleepy and answered with a muffled "Okay." What could Luis be talking about?

"I want you to know before you get to work. It's a plan Cy has hatched up. There's a guest in suite 3. If I'm right, he's going to make a proposition to you."

"Okay, thanks," Joe said, too sluggish to process this whispered information. He needed more sleep. Last night had been too short. After dinner, things had heated up. Not a surprise. Oscar was the key, Joe reflected even in his haze.

"Talk to me when you get here," Luis said, hanging up.

Joe looked at his phone, surprised the call had ended so abruptly. Anyway, his mind was now starting to focus, and the sex memory was flowing through him. He opened the front door for some fresh air. A deep breath made him feel better about facing another day with a new Cy trial. It would soon be over. Then Joe thought of Oscar and his reliance on Cy, and he became more concerned.

Back inside, he found that most of their clothes were left in a heap near the sofa. That's how their in-depth discussion ended last night—in a rush to nakedness.

Joe picked up his clothes, dressed quickly, and hurried outside to his car. He'd get back to Luis's apartment, shower, and put on fresh clothes. And he'd check his pill stash. It might be time for refills. Then he'd stop at Carl's Jr. for some coffee and head to Casa Vista Oro to discover what chaos Cy was now trying to stir into his life. Their life.

* * *

Joe saw Cy sitting upright as a sentinel at his office desk as he scurried past the window. Joe slowed a bit and sighed, briefly hunching his broad shoulders. He had to acknowledge Cy, so he bobbed his head and smiled but kept on toward the utility room. Joe needed to get more info from Luis about this new threat.

Joe's mind was astir. Was his boss's jealousy that deep and distressing? Luckily, Luis was sitting quietly in their little getaway room, sipping a cup of coffee, his head down and moving back and forth as if he were contemplating some thorny tragedy.

"Luis, I'm here a little early," Joe said, making his greeting a thank-you.

Luis seemed more anxious than usual, especially given his long familiarity with Cy's hijinks. Joe knew immediately that this particular ploy really rankled him.

"What's up?" Joe asked, settling his butt on a low storage cabinet across from Luis.

Luis quickly glanced out the door.

"The guest in suite 3 is an old friend of Cy's and Matt's. He helped them when they were first getting started here, after Bono became mayor and the city began to let gays develop guesthouses. Before Casa Vista Oro became a boutique guesthouse."

"Okay," Joe said, turning to look outside the door also to make sure they wouldn't be overheard. He had picked up Luis's anxiety.

Luis smiled briefly. Something amused him about the next part.

"They shot porn here. You would barely recognize that the place is the same now. The porn was shot mostly by the pool. It's still available on the guest's company website. I overheard him telling Cy it was some of his best-selling work. Something about the naïveté of his approach."

Joe kept nodding, not knowing why this was a threat. Surely Cy didn't hope to recruit Oscar into the porn trade. Joe knew Cy had too much care for Oscar. That was the heart of the problem.

"I don't see why this guy's presence should be a problem."

Luis continued to smile, a Cheshire cat smile. "Cy canceled a paying customer to bring this guy in. It was all last-minute. He told me to be sure that you cleaned the guy's room."

Luis leaned forward and stared into Joe's eyes as if he were checking whether Joe had gotten the point.

Luis's point suddenly dawned on Joe. Was this guest supposed to be recruiting him? Joe chuckled, then covered his mouth, looking again out the open door to see if Cy was sneaking about.

"Do you mean this guy is supposed to recruit me? To do a porno?" Joe asked, hardly able to keep the amazement from his voice.

Luis nodded his head. "That's what I think. Why else bring the guy here and ask me to have you clean his room?"

Joe stared at Luis in disbelief.

"You know it's about money, don't you?" Luis said, breaking into his thoughts. "Cy knows you're going to need cash. This guy will offer it. That's the bait. He baits the trap with cash."

Joe's eyes grew larger and glinted with understanding. Ah. That made sense. Cy would dangle cash in front of him, see if he'd sell his soul.

Joe had watched porno but had never thought about the souls of the guys who did it. Another flaw in his priesthood, he supposed. He had assumed it was all mechanical, young men doing what young men do. Could he even pass muster as a porn star? The question made him want to laugh.

"You're smiling," Luis said, now sounding stern.

Joe felt the sting. Luis thought he should take this seriously.

"I don't see myself as porno material," Joe said. "It sounds ridiculous to me."

"Cy doesn't want to make you a star. He wants to make you less desirable to Oscar. He thinks—or maybe he knows—that Oscar likes you because you are a man with ideals. Oscar is a young man with ideals, a young man scrambling to find a place, to get stability in his life. Cy helps provide that. He doesn't want you to provide it. You or Edward. It's love, I suppose, Cy's love for Oscar," Luis said, setting his cup down and rising. "I just wanted to warn you."

"Thanks...thanks," Joe said, breaking out of a bizarre reverie, thinking of Oscar and Edward and how they'd react if he did a porno. After all, the three of them did need money—a lot of money—they needed a down payment, even two months' rent. Cy, the expert, knew how to bait the trap.

* * *

The man from suite 3 found Joe in the breakfast nook later that morning. Joe was checking the coffee urn and turned around to see a fit older white man, skin leathered from the sun, wearing shorts and a tank top that revealed a worked-out body. Short-cropped gray hair. No wrinkles on his face. A static smile. He approached and put a hand on Joe's shoulder.

"Good morning," he said. "Glad you're checking the coffee supply. I need as much rocket fuel as I can get to propel me out of the morning doldrums."

The man's hand remained on Joe's shoulder, massaging him gently. As Joe stepped back, the man from suite 3 took his hand away and extended it in greeting. "Derrick, here," he said, offering as much smile as his tight face would allow.

Joe took Derrick's hand and found himself in a firm handshake that Derrick held for longer than Joe considered comfortable. Pointing to his badge, he said, "Joe. Let me know if you need more coffee. I'd be happy to brew it up for you."

"Glad to hear that," Derrick said, finally releasing Joe's hand.

They stood a moment in silence. Joe was feeling his muscles tense and his breath shorten as the older man examined him. There was no shame in Derrick's gaze. He stood back a bit to take in all of Joe. He seemed pleased with what he saw.

"Let me know if you need anything," Joe finally said, hoping to extricate himself from this awkwardness.

Derrick merely grinned in response and went to sit out by the pool where two younger guests were already frolicking in the water.

* * *

Cy had left the perch near his office window and was relaxing outside on his small nook of a patio tucked away from the pool and spa, a place where special guests often congregated for the best cocktails and evening hors d'oeuvres. His rock fountain was burbling, spreading water over the surface of the stone. An aloe plant was in blossom with a hummingbird visiting it at that very moment.

This is heaven, Cy thought. He had achieved so much here in Palm Springs. And now he was about to make a crucial move in maintaining Oscar as his own project.

The priest. He should never have offered him work and shelter. The thought of his mistake ruffled his morning bliss. Then he heard movement.

Derrick had arrived. Old Derrick looking in great repair. The man was obsessive. But that didn't bother Cy. They'd been good for each other. Cy would feed Derrick talent and Derrick would send Cy his discoveries for a night or two of pleasure. And there had been those early days when Derrick had paid very well to use the guesthouse for his most significant films. Those were the days!

But now! No porno here. Cy had cultivated a different clientele, people who could lose big at the casino one night and still plan another late-night outing the next evening.

His kind of spenders.

"Have a seat," Cy said, gesturing to the lounge chair next to him.

"Happy to," Derrick replied, settling into the chair. "We've got business to discuss. Can we do it here?"

"We're good here," Cy said. He had told Luis to keep Joe busier than normal today. He wanted to tire him. And keep him visible to Derrick.

Cy asked, "Have you met him yet?"

Derrick nodded. "At the breakfast nook."

Cy smiled. Derrick didn't comment further on Joe. So much like a business negotiation. Never give anything away, even your first impressions. Barter for everything.

"Good," Cy said. "And I hope your suite is adequate. You haven't been with us for a while."

"No, no, I haven't. And the suite is certainly up to your standards."

Cy smiled again and decided to remain silent. He and Derrick had already discussed Cy's idea over an evening phone call. Cy had suggested a porno series with ex-priests and ex-pastors and ex-rabbis set in Palm Springs and shot in an exotic space; he had a Moroccan villa in mind. The men had to be in good shape—and desperate.

They would publicize the series online with trailers and brief bios, pictures from the guys' pasts—something to give it validity. Derrick had seemed interested. It wasn't your typical guy-in-a-collar sex shoot. They'd bring in pictures from the guys' previous careers, like reality TV. The videos would stir controversy.

Of course, it could ruin some of these guys. But that was the goal. Ruining lives. Really only one life.

* * *

Derrick smiled as Joe came over to his table near the coffee urn to remove the lunch dishes.

"Everything was good?" Joe asked, offering a smile but feeling off base.

A thought kept churning through his mind, disturbing the previous calm. Could he really be considering porn as a way to make money? What had become of him?

Derrick nodded, putting down *The New Yorker* he'd been reading. "Everything was good," Derrick said as he rose from his chair. He took a couple of steps toward Joe, placed an arm across Joe's shoulder, and spoke quietly into his ear, "Can you come see me in my suite when you have a moment?"

"Is there a problem?" Joe asked.

"No problem. Something I'd rather discuss in private," Derrick said. He then took his hand away from Joe's shoulder and headed inside. "I'll be working inside for a while. I look forward to speaking with you."

Joe hurried away with the dishes, forgetting to wipe the small table. He was looking down and shaking his head, barely able to watch his step. He had to come back to Derrick's room. He had to comply with a guest's request.

He headed to the utility room, his oasis at Casa Vista Oro.

Joe had the small sink to himself. He stacked all the luncheon plates and started cleaning them. Luis was off tending to the koi pond. It had been their routine now for months. But Joe's mind was on Derrick's room. And on the threesome's project, for which they needed cash.

Joe dawdled over the dishes but finally finished them. Luis had stopped in to see if he needed help. Joe knew there was more in Luis's question. Surely he had seen Derrick's whisper. Joe knew Luis's opinion about the porn route: Luis was against it.

But, to his surprise, Joe was considering it. He would do anything to keep his new dream from failing.

Yet as a founder, he needed to be careful. He could lose his grip on the dream. And then what? Become an object of derision, just as he had become back home?

He wiped his hands and felt the sweat gather in his armpits. This was another one of those defining moments.

And he was close to a conclusion.

Joe knocked on Derrick's door, which had been left ajar.

"Come in," Derrick yelled from the master bedroom. Derrick's accommodation was one of the larger suites with a living room, galley kitchen, and two bedrooms. The master had an interior patio, planted in succulents on one wall and a waterfall rippling over a section of stacked stone in the corner. Either Derrick had money to splurge, Joe assumed, or Cy had rewarded his old friend with a couple of nights in the pleasure palace.

Joe walked in warily, standing in the doorway for a moment.

Still no Derrick.

Joe wasn't going to head into the master bedroom. He turned to open the louvers of the plantation shutters. He wanted the conversation to be in the living room, exposed, as they'd be, to the courtyard, almost in public.

Derrick called again. "I'm on the patio. Come on back, if you don't mind."

Joe shook his head. Just what he didn't want. He exhaled deeply, sighing. Then he thought if Oscar could walk in on strangers, offering his relaxed presence, then Joe should be able to do this. It would be something like the confessional, except there could be a naked man back there.

Joe walked toward the patio.

At the bedroom door, he saw that Derrick was lying on one of two lounge chairs in the patio. He was wearing a cherry red thong and seemed slathered in suntan lotion. He had a stack of papers next to him as if he'd been catching up on business affairs.

"I'm getting my vitamin D," Derrick said, having noticed Joe edge into the bedroom. "Come and lounge with me for a second. It won't take long."

Joe's eyebrows arched with curiosity and worry.

* * *

Edward was home feeling abandoned. Joe was at work. Oscar had a client. Edward was washing the sheets.

Did this scenario presage his new life?

The life of a domestic.

The daddy at home.

That scenario wasn't the fulfillment of his dreams.

He decided to take a few moments off from housework and went out for a stroll around the grounds. He'd check which plants were flowering. Check whether there was a cloud in the sky hovering over the mountain.

And he'd clear his mind. After all, last night had left it cluttered with images. Images and scents. Hair everywhere he reached. And the tautness of young muscles.

It was damn great!

That's what he'd felt about last night, but after momentarily reliving the high, his worries began. Was it another one-night wonder, or could they make this work? The three of them. Day in and day out.

Edward decided he needed some help sorting through his thoughts. He'd reach out to an old pal. He'd call Pascal.

With the call in mind, he stopped at pool number one, went over to check the water temperature, and then headed home. Edward wanted quiet for this call. Quiet and the protection of four walls from listening ears.

Edward checked his watch as he approached the condo's front patio. Pascal was probably at the drop-in center, making coffee, and chatting with the homeless who headed there for relief from the weather and for the possibility of a warm drink and a sugary breakfast. A safe place filled with aimless banter or welcome silence. Pascal had a cell phone now, a gift from Edward so Pascal would be easier to contact.

Edward unlocked the condo door and headed to the sofa. How to start this call?

"Pascal, can you talk?"

Pascal had answered on the second ring.

"Sure, sure. I'm just taking a break. Perfect timing. We're having a gorgeous late-fall day. Too bad you're not here!"

"So you're outside? Able to chat a while?"

"You know me! I'm outside on the sidewalk meandering through the neighborhood. What's up, sweet man?"

"I need some advice. I wish you were here on the sofa with me," Edward said, then grinned when he thought of what the sofa had become—a site for the threesome to gather, interlocked and playful.

"And I assume advice for something other than spiritual since you have our Fr. Joe for that recourse."

Edward grinned again, more broadly. Pascal was playing with him, which usually delighted Edward. Pascal was direct, much like Oscar. Pascal had chosen to live out loud, in public, a happily gay man on an exacting spiritual path.

"Things have gotten complicated here," Edward said, still figuring out what to say. "I seem to be in a unique kind of relationship."

"You're not chained up somewhere, are you?" Pascal asked, chuckling.

Edward remained silent. He wanted to move beyond camp. Was Pascal the right guy to talk to? Edward wrinkled his forehead and took a deep breath, then exhaled sharply.

"Sorry," Pascal said. "This is serious. Go ahead. I won't joke anymore."

"Thanks." Edward swallowed and jumped right in. "Things have heated up here, and I don't mean weather-wise. I've had sex with Joe."

Edward paused. He was sure Pascal had expected something dishy about Kenny to be the first item in an update. But Kenny had dwindled into a blip on the horizon. New stars were rising in Joe's firmament and Edward's star was blazing bright.

"And there's a third man. A young man, Oscar—you've heard us mention him, I'm sure. He does massage for a living. He's very mature. And we're all planning to live together. As a throuple, I think you'd say."

That was it. The facts. But the facts lacked his feelings, his hope for this arrangement. And the facts lacked his fear and the sense of foreboding that they were heading out onto an ocean in a ship without rudder or compass. Edward slouched deeper into the sofa and bit his upper lip.

"So you're like a small community," Pascal said, quick in his response, "like a Catholic Worker house except without the prayer and service part. Or maybe there is that. Oh, and there's more of that frowned-upon sex part. At least I hope so..."

Edward sat up a bit and smiled. Pascal had just described the Palm Springs life Edward was starting in Pascal's own terms. And this life didn't seem odd to Pascal. It took a form Pascal understood.

Of course, the three of them weren't forming a religious fraternity. Not in any formal sense. But they were a fraternity, only with a different bonding agent. Not just common interests or common goals, but love. Carnal love, yes, but also love of each other's presence, each other's soul. At least a starting version of that.

* * *

Joe stood in the patio where a deeply tanned Derrick lay sunbathing. Derrick smiled up at him and gestured toward the other lounge chair.

"Don't worry, Cy won't see you here."

Joe blinked his eyes with an irritated flutter. Did everyone assume he was just another wide-eyed creature caught in Cy's net? Had he begun to give off a scent of helplessness?

"So, do you know about my history with Cy and Matt?" Derrick asked after Joe had settled into the lounger. The umbrella above him provided shade for Joe's eyes; still, he squinted a bit, wondering how this conversation would go.

"I've heard that you shot pornos here when they first bought the place."

Derrick nodded his head, then chuckled. "I made my first pile of money in porn, just at the tail end of the 'Golden Age' with home video propelling erotic tapes into bedrooms—and living rooms. I still dabble in porn, so I guess, I'll always be known for video sex. It's like an identifier that's been branded on me. And it's true I paid Cy and Matt good money to film here. They used that money to make improvements, upgrade the space. They came to the desert without much capital, you know. It was Cy's hard work and real estate investing that propelled them into what I'd call the really comfortable set. But I knew them when they were scrambling. We scrambled together." He paused.

Joe could see Derrick was weighing his next words.

"So, I hear you were a priest," Derrick said, taking this conversation down the path Joe expected—the proposal for a porn film, probably starting with Joe in his Roman collar. Derrick smiled at him. "It's kind of like your identifier, the brand that's been seared onto your skin. No?"

Joe chuckled. "That's true. It usually comes up in most serious conversations. It's hard for me to...to explain myself without reference to it."

"I understand your situation," Derrick said, sitting up slightly in the lounger and hiking up his dark glasses, letting Joe look into his pale blue eyes. "I was a Trappist for five years. New Lamnay. Have you heard of it?"

Joe's mouth dropped open; his eyes flickered. Derrick's story had an unexpected plot twist. "Yes, I've been there, on retreat. Five years a monk. Wow! That's a good stay."

"I had been in rehab. I was a dopehead as a youth. Then I got clean and was looking for a way to stabilize, which I found as a monk. Then I found gay sex!" Derrick burst out in laughter.

"In the monastery?" Joe asked, the question jumping out of him.

"More like out in the fields." A dreamy look settled on Derrick's face.

Joe wanted to know more but, then, he saw a veil descend over Derrick's eyes, something he'd often experienced when dealing with parishioners who carried old deep wounds.

They sat in silence for a moment.

"I invest in some websites," Derrick said, lowering his Ray-Bans back down over his eyes. "Cy knows this. I'm a passive investor these days."

Joe held his breath, fearing that the offer was coming now.

"Cy has told me about your plans, the three of you. The other priest and the young guy."

Joe nodded, still holding his breath.

Derrick smiled, and for a moment, Joe thought Derrick was playing with him, teasing him.

"I've done a lot of things in life. Some good. Some bad." Derrick shifted again. "I'd like to do some good."

Joe cocked his head and held his body still. Where was this conversation going?

"You seem uncertain about my intent," Derrick said, leaving some sadness to hover for a moment. "I don't give off that old Catholic vibe, do I? You're having difficulty pegging me into the right social hole now."

Joe shifted, knowing he should engage more actively in the conversation, but he needed to look into Derrick's eyes, now hidden behind dark lenses. "You're right. I...to be honest...I thought we were going to talk about a porno you wanted to shoot."

Derrick broke out in laughter, trying to get the words out but spluttering too hard. Finally, he stopped. "I can't get away from it! I come off like a cocktail-swilling and porn-bingeing old queen, even though I spend an hour or so a day in meditation and read Merton regularly!"

Joe sat up, his cheeks reddening. "I'm sorry. I...I...you're right. I had you pegged as one type of person. I couldn't read you." He was so flustered now he wanted to get up and walk away.

Derrick had settled down, his face seeming more relaxed. At peace. He removed his glasses, maybe getting the drift of Joe's comment about "reading" him. "Your perception is partially true. I do love my porn." He smiled now. "And you'd probably do well as on-camera talent. But that's not what I want to talk about. I want to talk about this house you guys are looking for. And start-up funds."

Joe swore not to say anything until Derrick had checked out from Casa Vista Oro that afternoon. Neither of them wanted a scene with Cy.

"He'll come around," Derrick had said as they made plans for the house. "But it could be rocky for a while. I'll stonewall him, not saying anything about the real topic of our meeting. Eventually, I'll come clean."

Joe had wanted to cut his ties to Cy, but Derrick told him to hold off on that. "He's not a total asshole, like some guys with money and power. He does help people. You might be surprised."

So that was the message he'd bring home, that and Derrick's willing offer to finance the house or houses, to help pay for Oscar's training, and to support their first clients after they had opened for business.

* * *

The three of them had a quick dinner, roasted eggplant with lemon and a side of penne. Edward had insisted it was cool enough to use the oven again, but the condo had still gotten hot. So after dinner the threesome went for a dip in the pool and returned to gather in the front patio, circling their white plastic patio chairs so each set of eyes could watch the others.

Joe was particularly happy, actually giddy. All had agreed that Derrick's offer was remarkable. So unexpected.

"I'll phone him tomorrow to say that we accept his offer," Joe said after they had been settled for a while. Their feet were mixed together in the center. Joe felt a bonding he'd never before experienced. It was something like a family feeling. Something tribal. Positively sexual. Maybe blessed.

Author's Note

Palm Springs is a unique place in this world. Aside from its desert beauty, it and its neighboring cities have become the home for a large gay, lesbian, bisexual, and transgender population. Often these are retirees. And a significant number of these retirees are long-term survivors of HIV.

Why come to Coachella Valley (home to Palm Springs)? Partly because of the presence of peers. No one needs to be in the closet in Palm Springs. Aside from LGBT social institutions, there is healthcare that acknowledges and is sensitive to this diverse population. If you're HIV, writing "HIV" on your intake documents is not unusual. I don't know the actual percentage of HIV people in the Coachella Valley, but it's substantial. Substantial enough to keep HIV care practitioners booked.

When I first came to the Valley, I saw a documentary titled *Desert Migration,* which explores the lives of a group of men with HIV who had moved to the Coachella Valley. Without predicting the future, for the moment the "migration" is a fact. So, although Fr. Joe Tierney is not initially motivated by a search for a comfortable place to be HIV positive, he lands in a place that is welcoming to the infected.

Today, many of these men and women who are long-term survivors are forming social groups. Institutions are responding with educational events, counseling, and studies of this population.

Also, I don't have figures for the number of people who live in polyamorous relationships. In my experience, such relationships are not uncommon in the Palm Springs gay community. Stay long enough in the Valley and you'll hear someone say "They're a throuple." And relationships, partnerships, and marriages between individuals of different ages are as common as a lineup at any bar for Friday Happy Hour.

This novel takes place in the mid-2000s before the iPhone. It is only a few years from the 2000 *Kansas City Star* exposé on "AIDS in the Priesthood," the motivating event that caused me to write *Father Tierney Stumbles.* The novel does not tell any real person's story. It is entirely made up. Most of the institutions, restaurants, and bars mentioned in this novel existed in 2005 or began by 2010. The guesthouse Casa Vista Oro is a figment of my imagination, as is the character Cy. I have stayed in several guesthouses in Palm Springs and have never met anyone like Cy. The apartment and condo complexes in this novel are also figments of my imagination, but ring true to my experience or to tales I have heard.

The military policy of "Don't Ask Don't Tell" ended in September 2011. By 2008, however, the Pentagon had dismissed 12,000 officers. Lieutenant Wylands was still at threat by the policy. I chose not to focus on it. Numerous lawsuits were lodged against the policy. People resisted.

Finally, I wish to thank my friend and fellow resident of Palm Springs, Alan Zimmerman, for his willingness to read and critique this novel in progress. I appreciate his insights and hope I did them justice.